CORN, COWS, AND THE APOCALYPSE

A Nebraska Apocalypse Novel

FELICIA JEDLICKA

For all those who believed and especially those who didn't.

More titles by FELICIA JEDLICKA

DESTINY REJECTED
DESTINY RECLAIMED
DESTINY RAZED
DESTINY RESTORED

DÉJÀ VU

SAVE THE HUMANS

THE NECROMANCER'S CHILD

SISTER WITCHES
THE DEVIL'S SHADOW
THE DEVIL'S SOUL

THE NEBRASKA APOCALYPSE NOVELS
CORN COWS AND THE APOCALYPSE
COW TIPPING AFTER THE APOCALYPSE
CORN HUSKING AFTER THE APOCALYPSE

THE WARDEN SERIES
SUCCESSORS
RIVALS
LOVERS AND LIARS
BAD BLOOD
TENANTS AND TYRANTS
THE RING BEARER
GODS AND MONSTERS
BEASTS AND BURDENS
MAGIC AND MAYHEM
FORK IN THE ROAD
DETAILS AND DEADLINES

Corn, Cows, and the Apocalypse

Prologue

"THIS IS JIMMY THE Card coming to you live from the end of the world. Cheer up, all you ungodly rejects, we are free from the anarchy that *was* civilization. So, take the nooses off your necks, and the barrels out of your mouths, and rejoice in the rebirth of the new world.

"In case you've been living under a rock, or just hiding in your house like a crazy cat lady, you should know those saintly silver sonsabitches playing possum in your yard are coming back...*with a vengeance*.

"Those conniving bastards are *not*, I repeat, *not*, coming to bless you, take you to heaven, or pander their religious beliefs to you. They are coming to *kill* you. So, people of the Metro and anyone close enough to hear this broadcast: STOP TRYING TO INTERACT WITH THEM! They are bad. Run. *Run away.*"

This is the End, or is it the Beginning?

SO, THE APOCALYPSE CAME.

It wasn't nearly as impressive as the religious gurus said it would be. There wasn't any fire or brimstone. The seas didn't boil, and the skies didn't fall. There wasn't even a bad storm or an earthquake. If the four horsemen were scheduled for it, they must have gotten lost on the way. Aside from 4.2 billion men, women, and children simultaneously falling over dead across the globe, there really wasn't anything to mark the moment.

If you must know, it was on August 22nd at 8:46 a.m. Nothing significant about the numbers. Nothing special about the day. It was kind of disappointing.

Don't get me wrong, seeing everyone around me suddenly drop dead definitely spiked my *WTF*-scale, and the deafening silence that followed caused an uproar in my brain that threatened my sanity. But once the panic attack subsided, it was all just a matter of letting go of any preconceived ideas I had about the rest of my life.

Post-apocalyptic life is a lot like retirement. You don't have to work anymore, you get to take lots of naps, and there's no reason to worry about the future, because you're probably going to die soon anyway.

The key to avoiding the suicide-garnering boredom of a life without purpose is keeping busy. The saying goes, "Idle hands are the devil's playground." In the godless aftermath of the reckoning, that statement is gospel. Or maybe it already was. Sorry, I'm a little behind on my Bible readings. *Obviously*, since I'm still here.

Religion had always ranked pretty high for my friends and neighbors. Church on Sundays, soup suppers, and fish fries were the core of social networking for our farming community. I, on the other hand, found the entire religious structure to be manipulative, dogmatic, and bigoted.

After that catastrophic day, most of my home town's population of 20,000 remained right where they fell, in a surreal crystalline state. The bodies didn't rot, but their skin took on an unmistakable silvery sheen. The *apocagees*—apocalyptic refugees—started calling them the "crystalline dead," the "silver saints," and eventually they gained the name "glimmer grim."

I'm not going to bore you with the three months of emotional plateaus and speed bumps that led me to the realization that I was not just *feeling* alone in the world, but I actually was. I also won't detail my intense self-flagellating prayer sessions, which, let's face it, was kind of like trying to un-bake a cake. To sum it up—for those of you hoping for an honest, meaningful discussion about the trials and tribulations of someone dealing with the end of the world—I cried... a lot.

When I thought life couldn't get any worse, the crystalline dead started to animate. I won't use the Z-word to describe their behavior, but I will say they did not have good intentions. There was a lot of talk about their sudden resurgence being a miracle—that's when the "silver saints" designation became popular. Unfortunately, soon after, it became clear the mobile corpses were hosts to puppeteering demons that wanted to kill, rape, maim, and—well, you know—all the stuff that makes a devil's playground into a carnival of carnage.

It was around that same time I met up with three crazy apocagees from Chicago. On that particular day, I was in the process of having my arms broken by one of the glimmer grim. No one I knew, but he looked like a nice old man. Had he not been dead and possessed by a demon, I imagine he might have offered me an ice tea upon passing his home, instead of tackling me like a football player.

I'd like to say I was putting up a good fight, or I had gotten a good hit in before he got the better of me, but alas I am not the heroine you seek. I'm not even the sidekick in this one. I'm not even the sidekick's sidekick. I'm more like the kickstand. If the heroine rode around on a horse, I would be the one to hang out in the stables and guard it—which is funny, since as the kickstand rather than the sidekick, I wouldn't even have the skills to stop a horse thief.

Anyway, I digress. One of the three apocagees, August Smith, rescued me from the glimmer grim. It might have been the angle of the sun, or the fact I had lost a significant amount of oxygen from screaming like a ninny, but August seemed to radiate light the first time I saw her.

To thank her for her heroic gesture, I passed out against her. When I woke up she was holding me in the bed of a pickup truck on its way down Highway 81. She smiled down at me, and pushed the hair out of my face as it whipped into my eyes. She said something—a greeting of some kind. But I couldn't hear it over the rumble of the Dodge. I didn't say anything back. I just stared at her. I looked into her eyes through my snarled hair, and I wondered if it was possible to have love at first sight in a platonic version.

When the formal introductions were over, I gave them the short version of my life story, and August invited me into her group. I didn't even consider any other options. She was now my heroine, and I was her third sidekick. I may not have had any horses to guard, but I had damsel in distress written all over me, and August was always going to be there to save me.

Or so I thought.

RoadKill

T HE ROAD HOME FROM the Big O was littered with stalled vehicles from the people who died in transit. I hung onto the roll bar for dear life while the truck weaved in and out of the stilled traffic. I let out a "woo-hoo," joining a cacophony of "woo-hoos" from my female partners flanking me in the back of the black pickup truck.

August, on my right, was the living incarnation of Xena, the Warrior Princess. In addition to her height, the striking long chocolate hair, and facial features akin to a biracial, she had muscles that would put a good number of men to shame. She was the leader of our little group and we were all happy to follow her without question.

Until I met her, I had no idea how much I needed a friend. August was a strong woman mentally and physically, but socially she was gentle and nurturing. Despite her lethal skill set, she exuded something undeniably peaceful. She was what held us all together when the world threatened to pull us apart.

Haden Summers, on my left, was for all intents and purposes August's first sidekick. She was an intense woman with straight muddy blond hair down to her shoulders. She was loud, arrogant, forceful, and a little bit crazy, but she made things fun.

The truck jerked around another car, threatening my foothold. Haden braced herself on the bedside to yell around into the driver's side window. "Is that the best you can do?" she yelled over the wind that was swallowing her words.

She was given a meaty fist with a raised middle finger from the driver as her answer. She laughed and pulled back. August slammed her hand against the roof a couple times and the truck slowed down.

Devin Reed, our designated driver, was August's second sidekick. He was a brawny young stud who could have made his living as a model in his pre-apocalyptic life. His tawny waves and chiseled Kirk Douglas chin were too much to resist, let alone his disarming charm.

Devin was a reckless thrill seeker with a knack for driving and fighting in the new world. Speeding through the melee of traffic was his favorite part of our trips into and out of the city. He loved dodging through the metal obstacle course as fast as his pickup would take him. As he put it: That's what a *Dodge* is named for.

Devin slid open the back window and handed out three football helmets. August passed one to each of us. We put them on and inserted the attached mouth guards. When we were all properly protected from concussions and broken teeth, we took a firm grip of the roll bar. August hammered her fist on the roof, signaling to Devin we were ready.

The truck picked up speed until it reached the off-road section in the highway. Through the many trips to the Metro, we had managed to push or pull the most obtrusive vehicles out of our way so we had a clear path to and from. Unfortunately, one particular spot on the highway was an absolute mess: Too many overturned semi-trucks and not enough room to get by.

Instead of weaving through, Devin veered off the road into a cornfield that bore the tracks of our many trips. The rutted ground sent vibrations through my arms, and it was all I could do to hold on. Haden yelled and hooted as she released one hand to ride her bull like a real cowboy. I admired her spirit, but sometimes I thought she had a death wish.

Truth be told, I think we all did. There's nothing quite like being the last one picked for a cosmic game of dodgeball. I didn't know much about the guidelines for inclusion in the end of days, but I was pretty sure I got the shaft. Most of the people left behind were either outright atheists or devil worshipers in some form or another. One of the exceptions to the *most* was me. I was never really religious, but I certainly wasn't an atheist.

However, I learned admitting you aren't an atheist is a bad idea. People tend to look poorly on you, as if you're trying to be better than them. I've even seen people get stoned for such anti-heresy.

Since God rejected us, there was only one thing we could do to fill the emptiness we all felt: Embrace the apocalypse with open arms and pretend we didn't give a crap about heaven, angels, and fluffy clouds. It was the sour grapes theory at its best. So instead of sulking or slowly descending into madness, we tried to have as much fun as possible.

Since the new world was basically the old world, just with fewer people, it was easy to find something to keep us entertained. There were enough people left to keep basic utilities functional. Driving was never an issue because the demand for fossil fuels plummeted to record lows. Food was readily available at the supermarket as long as you could tolerate the smell of moldy vegetables and rotten meat.

Shopping was a dream come true. Money was no longer a functional exchange method, so we took whatever we wanted. Poetically, all the things I thought I wanted when I was a minimum-wage grocery checker didn't matter when there wasn't endless advertising telling me to want it.

There was even a radio station broadcasting rock music in addition to the witty repartee of *Jimmy the Card*. He kept the tri-state area population up-to-date on the grim movements, as well as letting us know where we could get fresh fruits and vegetables. His radio program had become as central to our lives as our favorite television shows used to be.

The truck came to the end of the off-road path and we ramped back up onto the highway. My feet flew out from beneath me and I let out a squeal I tried to pass off as a "*wee!*" August laughed and helped me back up.

Devin punched the roof and August took her helmet off to poke her head in the back window. He told her something and she retracted to look down at the road ahead. She turned to us and nodded forward. "Grim straight ahead."

I peered over the roof and saw the shiny skinned corpse standing on the highway. Unlike the things that go bump in the night, the grim were not opposed to making daytime appearances. Though they generally did most of their major movements at night, they could turn up whenever the desire to harm a living being arose—which was pretty often.

"Oh, yeah." Haden removed her helmet and picked up a baseball bat from the truck bed. "This one's mine." She poised herself over the wheel well and tried a few practice swings. Her face contorted with the grin of a predator about to sink her teeth into her prey. It was all a game to her, but I was still getting used to the idea of hunting the glimmer grim for sport.

As we passed it, Haden slammed her bat into the corpse. Satisfying pink shards erupted from the creature's head like candy from a piñata. She raised her hands over her head triumphantly, while August and I cheered her on, and Devin honked the horn in approval.

All in all, life after the apocalypse was pretty good for us.

Clean Up in Aisle Five

I couldn't help but smile as we reached the tail end of our journey. The sign at the city limits of my hometown had long since been vandalized, but the remaining motto still held at the bottom: Power and Progress. It was a torturous reminder of how little power mattered, and how useless our progress had been.

In a town composed mostly of glimmer grim, we couldn't actually live inside the city limits. Not all the bodies were animated, but you never knew where an attack would come from, so it was best to avoid the most populated areas. However, we still needed supplies and we had picked clean the surrounding small-town grocery stores.

So, into my home sweet home we went, to pick up our stock for the week. That's where I came in. I was the third sidekick, Lenore Evans. Aside from guarding horses, the job of the third sidekick was essentially to gather supplies, cook, clean, and when necessary, be bait.

Devin pulled the truck into the grocery store parking lot and let the engine run while he hopped out of the cab with a cluster of fabric grocery bags looped over his arm.

Yes, we were still green in the new world.

He came to the back of the truck and put down the tailgate. I moved to the edge and he raised his hands for me like I was a child too small to jump down. The truck had a high clearance, but nothing I couldn't handle. His insistence on helping all of us down, however, was not about necessity. It was his modernized version of chivalry.

I crouched down and put my hands on his shoulders. He grabbed me around my waist, lifted me off the truck, and set me on the concrete. "Hmm, you've lost weight." He winked at me.

I probably hadn't lost any weight, but it's what every girl wants to hear after a big strong man puts his hands around her. "I stopped eating just for you," I teased.

"Not too much, though. I like to have something to grab," he teased right back.

I bit my lip, trying not to smile as big as my mouth wanted to. "Where's the list?" I changed the subject so my cheeks wouldn't redden. I had a mad crush on Devin, but I was way too shy to act on it.

He wasn't the type of guy who pursued women. He was too pretty to ever have to lift a finger to get what he wanted. August had always told me he wasn't the exclusive property of anyone, and I should make my intentions known, but I was still stuck in the old-world tradition of one man, one woman.

Our under-populated world had left male-female relationships open to expansive definitions. Justifiably, for reasons of comfort, reciprocity, and sanity, Devin freely offered himself to any woman willing to knock on his door. It was the knocking on the door part I hadn't quite worked up the nerve for.

Devin pulled a paper list out of his back pocket and handed it to me. I gave it a quick once-over, stuck it in my front jeans pocket, and took the bags from him.

"Why don't you pick me up some lube while you're in there?" he requested.

"What kind?" I asked before I fully understood what he was asking for.

"Whatever kind makes you wet, baby." He grinned and hopped up on the tailgate.

I shook my head and walked off. There was no point getting hot and bothered now. Not when I had work to do.

I was the poster child for sidekicks, if I do say so myself. Sure, I was a glorified personal assistant/housekeeper, but I was damn good at it. I knew what brand of potato chips gave Haden the shits. I knew August loved Fig Newtons, but only the name brand version. I even knew Devin preferred the super thick and soft toilet paper.

Knowing about his toilet paper preference did take the edge off the massive crush I had on him, but only enough to keep me from embarrassing myself when he gave me attention. I may have barely qualified for the description *sexually active* before the apocalypse, but I wasn't stupid. I knew I wasn't the type of girl who could sleep around without tipping the scales of like and love. I would say it was because I was a romantic, but I think it had more to do with my profound neediness.

I raced through the aisles, shopping with the proficiency necessary to keep our stops in town as short as possible. With thousands of potentially animated grim, I didn't have the luxury of reading nutritional labels.

I picked out the right number of canned vegetables to last us a week, and the right number of canned fruits to keep us from eating every last sweet snack before the end of the day. Canned tuna and salmon were our meat staples, along with the occasional can of Spam, which, as it turned out, was a refreshing change from fish.

I spent a good deal of time experimenting with canned potatoes, and found I could conjure a meal reminiscent of a steak dinner. With the additions of canned soup, jarred sauces, pasta, crackers, nuts, and dried fruit, I had enough to keep us appeased for another week.

As I dared to cross by the putrid butcher section with my cart full of food, something caught my eye. Bearing in mind that corpses were scattered all around the store, I wasn't disturbed by the inactive bodies I had passed up to that point. However, the three bodies *standing* behind the meat counter were disturbing.

I did a double take as I passed and picked up speed with my cart. Three heads turned and watched me run through the back of the store.

Very disturbing.

"Crap. Crap. Crap," I babbled as the cart skidded around the corner of an aisle with me behind it. I picked up speed, closing in on the front doors, but before I could reach the end of the aisle a grim stepped out to block my path.

"Shit," I hissed and slid to a stop, using my body weight to slow down the cart's momentum. I looked back and the original three entered the aisle behind me. I was trapped.

"Shit," I concluded with the finality of a lazy surrender. I couldn't think of any way around them, aside from climbing the shelves, which I expected would result in me falling down in an avalanche of creamed corn.

I moved forward in hopes I could at least defend myself against the singular grim. August had been desperately trying to teach me self-defense, but I was so bad at it. Aside from being uncomfortable with physical confrontation, I was apparently the weakest female ever. I was average height and average build, which was a nice way of saying I was kind of short, and kind of scrawny.

I picked up one of my prepacked grocery bags and gripped it by the handles in one hand as I pushed my cart with the other. The grim at the end of the aisle limped toward me. I was relieved he was a new possession.

It took demons a couple weeks to get the hang of running the bodies. You could always tell which ones had been possessed for months. They had no trouble walking, running, and—God help us—talking. They usually didn't speak an understandable language when they did, but it was still unpleasant and so wrong to hear.

The grim jumped at me. I mustered the very smallest amount of courage and screamed out a ridiculous war cry as I swung my canned vegetables at the creature's head. He fell over with a dry dent in his skull.

I turned, prepared to celebrate my triumphant blow, but one of the other grim tackled me. I shrieked and fell back against the speckled white floor tiles. My head hit and I saw stars that matched the glittery skin of the man growling on top of me.

His hands gripped my throat, stifling my oxygen. He leaned his face close to mine and opened his mouth. I couldn't tell if he planned to bite me, molest me, or just kill me.

Either way, I was scared shitless, and it takes none of my pride to admit I screamed like a little girl. The creature withdrew, somehow offended by my noise. It only lasted a second though, and he was back in motion to bite, kiss, or whatever me.

Before I found out what his intent was, a bat crashed into his skull, chipping pieces of crystallized tissue and bone away. The remaining face turned and hissed at my heroine. August introduced it to her preferred weapon.

With a quick choreographed swipe, the samurai sword cut through the neck of the glimmer grim. The head dropped to the ground and the body flopped back on top of me. I pushed it away and stood up. I was so glad the bodies never bled. The crystallized features that gave them their first nickname went all the way through. They were essentially mummified, only they weren't desiccated so much as frozen... but without the cold.

"Grab the cart." August sheathed her sword and retrieved the bat.

"There's two more," I pointed out, surprised she hadn't noticed them.

"Those are yours, come on. Move fast." August ran ahead while I pushed the cart behind her. I looked back and saw the grim gaining. I couldn't understand why she didn't just finish them off. That's what she did.

When I said she was the heroine, I meant she always saved me. Anytime I was in trouble, I was going to be saved by her. Even when the circumstances seemed completely unrealistic to expect her to be there, she would suddenly arrive, as if she were psychically aware of my danger.

Where scrawny third sidekicks faced mortal danger, she would be there.

I pushed the cart onto the pitted concrete of the parking lot. August was already in the truck bed, having jumped the near three-foot height with the help of Devin's proffered knee. She grabbed my bow and arrow from our collection of weapons and got it ready.

I grimaced, thinking how stupid it was to do an exercise like this when I was in real danger. Devin gestured for me to get on with it. I rolled the cart to one side and ran to him. He lifted me as I pushed off the ground.

As I arrived on the tailgate, August handed me my loaded bow. The grim were nearly to the truck. Devin looked back at them anxiously as he handed Haden the grocery bags. I shot one arrow into the first glimmer grim. It was a dead-on bullseye to the heart. It wasn't enough to destroy the body, but it did disrupt the link with the demon, resulting in the appearance of *killing* the grim. August handed me another arrow and I hit the next grim in his eye. I reached for another one, and hit him in the other eye before he fell to the ground.

"How the fuck do you do that?" Haden glared up at me as she pulled the last bag of groceries in. "You can't hit a barn with a bullet, but that flipping thing, you're a surgeon with."

Devin slammed the tailgate harder than necessary. "I think the word you're looking for Haden, is *thanks*."

I couldn't help but smile at Haden's annoyance, but she was right. Aside from my youth-camp-instilled archery skill, I was virtually useless with weapons and fighting. Incidentally, it was my only outdoor-related talent, and I had never shot a living creature, outside of the glimmer grim, which by definition and debate weren't living.

Devin jumped back into the driver's seat and got us out of there before more grim arrived. I sat down against the back of the cab to enjoy the rest of the ride without my layered chestnut locks whipping me in the face. August sat down beside me and put her hand on mine.

"That was good, Lenore," she said proudly.

I shrugged. "Thanks." I often wondered if August would have even considered letting me into the group without my one small talent. She was so determined to teach me, like I was a liability to her if I couldn't defend myself. That was probably true, but at what point did she admit squeezing water from a stone was a waste of time?

"Just ignore her." August nodded to Haden who was sitting on the wheel well pouting. "You know how much she likes to be the center of attention."

"Yeah, I know. I just wish she'd let me have my little corner of the stage. It's all I have, you know."

August's eyes flickered over my face, reading more than my expression. "You are so much more than a corner," she said earnestly.

I shrugged again. It wasn't the first time she had tried to cheer me up with a you-are-the-light-of-the-world style compliment, but it always made me uncomfortable. I wasn't more than a corner of the stage, and I was okay with that. When she said I was worth more, it was as if she was saying I wasn't good enough as I was.

"Did you get everything before they attacked?" she asked, taking her hand away from mine. The cold vacancy that was left when she pulled away made me feel alone even though she was still sitting right next to me.

"Yes," I answered.

"Good. Haden, toss me my Newtons." Haden rolled her eyes, but searched through the bags for the comfort food.

While August devoured a handful of fruited cake, I flipped around and poked my head into the cab. Devin peeked over from his driving and smiled.

Damn, he was beautiful.

"Hey, cutie, what's up?" he asked.

"Nothing, I just wanted to see your smile," I said, trying to control my own smirk.

"Well, it's yours anytime you want it." He winked and offered his best photographic smile. I giggled and pulled my head back out. The introspective smile I kept on my face only incited more glares from Haden. Despite Devin being *public* property, she didn't like anyone enjoying his company, platonic or otherwise.

Spam...a lot

T EN MINUTES OUTSIDE OF the city, we pulled into our current residence, a four-bedroom, two-story house, sitting on roughly an acre of land. There were several outbuildings, sheds, and a two-car garage we never used, because it didn't lend itself to an easy escape.

Devin backed into the driveway and brought the truck as close to the house as he could without ruining the sidewalk. He killed the engine and hopped out to help us off the tailgate. He helped August first, who thanked him politely before heading into the house. He made it a point to drag Haden down his body as he set her down, which prompted her to give him a wet, sensual kiss.

I moved to slip out of the truck without his help so I didn't disrupt them, but he snapped his fingers at me from behind Haden's head. She finally released him, dragging her hand down his chest as she went.

Once she was gone he looked at me. "What was that?" He crossed his arms and scolded me with a half-serious sternness I rarely saw on him.

"You were occupied," I mumbled.

"Temporarily. Come here." I let him help me down. I would have liked for him to give me the same attention he gave Haden, but there was no way to outright ask someone to fondle you.

I stepped back and smiled. I reached for a bag of groceries, which I knew would be met with reproach. He grabbed my wrist and pulled my hand away. "What are you doing? I'll get those."

I smiled. "It will be faster if I help you."

"I will get them," he said firmly before forcibly turning me around and pushing me to the house with a spank. I yelped for the sake of flirting, but he hadn't actually hurt me.

"Fine," I said as I headed into the house.

I admired Devin's devotions to his minor chivalries. The world had changed so much, but it was the little things that kept us all from becoming an excerpt from the *Lord of the Flies*. Devin would claim his manners were all flirtation, but I suspected he needed to do certain things to keep the world civil in his mind. Sure, it was just a bag of groceries, but when you're killing what look like human beings left and right, it's important to define how you treat the real people.

The front door was more or less the side door, since the house was positioned stupidly on the property. As a result, I entered straight into the kitchen.

I immediately started my prep work for supper, which was going to be spaghetti. There were a lot of spaghetti nights, post-apocalypse. We had the option of going hunting for fresh meat, but as you might imagine, modern conveniences left us all lazy. No one wanted to go find, shoot, skin, and process an animal when they could just have Spam-ghetti.

Devin dragged in all seven bags of groceries in one trip and set them on the floor. "Anything else?" he asked.

I wanted to tell him bringing the groceries in was the easy part, and if he really wanted to help he could put them away, but I didn't.

Kitchen duty was the job of the third sidekick. At least that's what I told myself.

"No, dinner should be ready in forty."

"Great, I'm starving. I don't suppose you would let me spoil my appetite a little?" He leaned on the counter beside the stove. The kitchen was relatively open to the living room, except for the stove and its gigantic exhaust vent that obscured the view.

"Go ahead, August already has the Newtons."

"Ooh, Newtons. Okay, August." Devin eyed August on the couch in the living room. She looked up at him, defensively hugging her bag of sweets. "Pass the cookies."

"They're not cookies," she mumbled over her full mouth with mock offense. "They're fruited cake."

"Yeah, whatever, cough 'em up." Devin went in after the cookies, which August playfully pulled from his grip a few times before giving in. Despite his enthusiasm he only took one and gave the rest back. He knew how much she enjoyed them, and wouldn't dare deprive her of her guilty pleasure.

They snuggled in beside each other on the couch, talking and laughing the way old friends always do. I watched them as I prepared supper. When I finally went out to call upstairs for Haden, I found them asleep against each other.

I debated waking them, but decided to put some extra water in the sauce and leave it on the burner to warm. After Haden and I finished stuffing our faces, we leaned back from the table to make room for our carb-bloated tummies.

Haden sipped on a beer, while I stuck with water. I wasn't much of a drinker, which is to say I never got the hang of it. Drunken Lenore was not the best party guest to have. Sure, I might loosen up and have more fun, but the end result would always be someone's ruined shoes. I stuck with water.

Haden eyeballed me from across the table. Our relationship was difficult to define. It was almost like I was the third wife in some polygamist family. I could sense she didn't like me, but she respected August enough not to make a big deal about it. In the end, it was all just jealousy, but she would never admit to that.

"So, have you fucked Devin yet?" she asked. She probably intended to start a round of gossipy girl talk, but it came off as an accusation.

I glanced into the living room to make sure Devin was still fast asleep against August's shoulder. I wished I had a Polaroid camera. I would have used the camera on my phone, but cell reception was so patchy we started relying on land lines instead. Plus, I wasn't about to take the time to go print it. No, Polaroid should have stuck around longer. They could have made a big comeback after the rapture.

"No, I haven't gotten around to that," I said finding a reason to stir the remaining three strands of spaghetti on my plate.

"Why not? He's really good," Haden insisted, contradicting her obvious jealousy.

"I..."

"It's not like we're a couple." *More denial.* "It's pointless to get wrapped up in monogamy. I mean crap, the world is at its end, so why bother?"

I nodded even though I didn't agree. I was obviously single to the truest extent of the word, but I still liked the idea of a man just for me. I was an idealist in a realist world. I didn't mention that as the reason I hadn't made a move on Devin.

"Should we wake them?" She nodded to the living room. I was about to say no, but Haden barked at them to wake up and eat.

August and Devin stirred and stretched from their nap. I rinsed my plate and headed outside for some air. I mostly wanted to be away from Haden. As much as she felt *I* was the dead leg to the group, I felt the same about her. She was the complete opposite of me. She was loud, direct, formidable, and confident. I, on the other hand... insert antonyms of your choice.

I sat down on the side porch, which wasn't anything more than a concrete stoop. The back—technically the front—door to the house had a small wooden porch, but it wasn't well lit, and frankly, I was scared of the dark. With good reason, since the glimmer grim trekked miles during the night hours in search of victims.

The sun was down already, but the air was still warm. Summer had brought lots of humidity, and plenty of mosquitoes. There wasn't enough bug spray in the world to combat these blood-suckers. The temperature overall was abnormally high for June. The Midwest was known for its weird inconsistencies in weather, but apparently there was a heat wave over the entire country, and possibly the world.

Jimmy the Card's callers believed the demon population was increasing the temperature. There had been many discussions about the impact of the black plague on planetary climate, and how our situation was the opposite. Temperatures were rising instead of dropping like they did after the massive population decline of the plague. Blah, blah, blah... it was hot.

I smacked a mosquito as Devin came out thumping his pack of cigarettes. "Hey, what did it ever do to you?"

"He bit me." I was surprised he came to this stoop. Unlike me, Devin wasn't afraid of the dark. He usually had his cigarette on the back porch.

"*She* bit you," he corrected before sitting down so close to me that I had to move so he didn't sit on my hand. "You're a country girl, you should know that."

"Yeah, I forgot."

He lit his cigarette and took a long drag before offering it to me. I didn't smoke, but he always offered anyway, the same way you offer cake to a woman who says she's dieting. You know she doesn't want it, but it still seems rude not to offer.

I started to shake my head, but instead I took the cigarette from him. Maybe I wanted to be rebellious, or maybe I just wanted to put my lips where his had been; either way, I was stupid enough to take a generous drag and inhale it.

When my coughing finally subsided, the only thing I had to show for my errant attempt at smoking—besides epically embarrassing myself—was getting the pleasure of Devin's hand rubbing my back.

As if she could sense our proximity, Haden chose that moment to interrupt. "Devin, your food is getting cold," she said, nodding for him to head in.

"Yeah, I imagine it is." He continued to rub my back. I was aware of the subtle change he made in the motion, to make it look more sensuous than comforting. He knew as well as anyone how jealous Haden got. He liked to play it against her. The more irritated she got, the more often she knocked on his door.

"Well?" She motioned inside.

"Well what? I'm having a conversation with Lenore." I looked away before I could catch Haden's glare and/or finger gesture, but judging by Devin's amusement, it must have been pretty severe. "Bitch," he murmured after the door slammed shut.

His hand slid off my back and for a moment he was content to smoke his cigarette. The pensive look on his face could have been any number of things, but Devin wasn't the type to share his thoughts with anyone, least of all me.

I hadn't realized I was staring at him until he looked back at me. His brown eyes fixed on mine, and I became aware of how close we were. I thought he might kiss me and I was paralyzed with fearful hope. That wasn't how it worked though. Devin didn't make advances. I had to make the first move.

"Thanks for dinner," he said.

"You're welcome." Devin hadn't thanked me for dinner before. "You haven't even tasted it yet."

"You do a lot for us," he said. I shrugged when I realized there weren't any words coming out of my half-open mouth. "You don't ask for much in return." I might have offered him another shrug since my voice box was still unresponsive, but he pushed back a lock of my hair and tucked it behind my ear, interrupting whatever logic I had left in my brain. "Do you need anything, Lenore?"

This was his version of making a pass. All I had to do was say "yes" now, and once again when he posed the next question. We would be making out in less than a minute.

My heart was slamming into my chest, and my face was so hot I could only imagine the tomato red finish it held. I hadn't been able to speak or move for at least 30 seconds, but it felt like minutes. I don't know what changed at the end of those 30 seconds; call it cowardice, call it the last vestiges of prudishness, but I shook my head and turned away from him.

"No, I'm good."

I wasn't good. I was lonely.

Not that it wasn't obvious, but Devin didn't push the matter. He sighed like he had given it his best, and snuffed out his cigarette. "Okay, let me know if that changes. You know where to find me. You want first watch tonight?"

"Yeah, sure," I said before he went in.

I sat out on the stoop feeling more alone than when I started. I watched, listened, and waited for the glimmer grim to shuffle into the yard, attracted to the light like moths, but none came on my watch. They never did. Which was good, because if I couldn't stop a horse thief, how the hell was I going to stop a demon puppet?

Priest

HOLY WATER WAS AN important weapon against the glimmer grim. Although their preserved bodies were already sainted by God, the addition of holy water seemed to keep the demons from rising in them. I always kept a stash of it on hand in case we relocated to a new residence for the evening.

At the beginning of the apocalypse, when people still gave a damn about the corpses haphazardly lying around, houses were marked with the number of dead inside. Now the numbers stood as a warning. Any house with more than three dead was considered too dangerous to approach, day or night. The last thing you want is to go into an unknown closed space with four or more potential glimmer grim. Houses with two bodies were worth the risk. If they hadn't risen as demons yet, we locked them in the cellar or basement and routinely sprinkled them with holy water.

Our current home only had one resident basement dweller, and I had used up all my holy water to ensure he remained inert. That was why I had to go see Priest. His real name was Matthew Corte and it was a calculated decision to use the last of my holy water, because he was not the most pleasant man to socialize with.

Die a horrible painful death at the hands of a glimmer grim, or go see Priest to get more holy water? I assure you, there was a good, long debate.

How should I describe Priest? He was a loyal and dedicated servant of the Lord, until God left him behind with the rest of us ingrates. For a while, he believed God had left him for a purpose. His faith transcended to offer the residual population a path into the Lord's good graces, but let's face it, three months of preaching to people who don't want to look at a church, let alone pray in one, can wear you down.

So, Priest did something he had never done in his entire life. He got mad... at God. He rebelled against Him. Priest became a reformed man. Any inkling of his religious reserve was wiped away by drugs, alcohol, and sex. To add sacrilege to sacrament he screwed his endless harem of women on his church altar, while wearing his vestments. He even went so far as to graffiti his own church with heretical symbols—or maybe those were scribbles.

I couldn't blame him for his anger. I couldn't blame him for his desires either. However, for a man so high on God's chosen list, to fall so far, any respect I could have had for his position was reduced to pure pity. The man hadn't just fallen from his pulpit; he nosedived off it.

Priest sat on a wall, and had a great fall, but all the king's horses and all the king's men... couldn't have given a damn about putting him back together again.

Part of me wished I could fix him. It would have been nice to have someone to talk to about everything that had been going on. As I said, I'm not religious, but given that I was now living the end of days, it would have been nice to know what to expect.

I waited by the door to the church for a few minutes. I had learned the hard way that knocking and/or listening before entering his church was a wise choice. Priest certainly didn't mind the interruption, but there was still something inherently disturbing about pornographic imagery paired with a church background. Someone probably should have told Madonna that.

When nothing of a sexual nature sounded from within, I entered. It was only a small-town church: white wood siding, a steeple with a single bell, and not more than a dozen rows of pews inside. Priest had probably been on a meager income there.

I saw him sitting in the front row of pews with his back to me. If I hadn't known any better I would have thought he was praying, but I was disappointed and disgusted when he let out a satisfied groan. I cursed under my breath and tried to sneak back out the door.

"Lenore?"

I cringed. "I'll come back."

"No need, I'm finished. Come in."

I turned back in time to see a young woman wiping her mouth and scurrying, abashed, out the door behind the altar. I shook my head and returned to the front row where Priest was now lounging in a euphoric haze. I sat down in an adjacent pew. He was all in black, except the white collar he refused to take off, despite it being significantly irreverent to his new lifestyle.

"I hope you didn't come for my services, I'm afraid I'm all used up for an hour or so."

I didn't give any hint of a smile at his joke. I couldn't tell if he was drunk, stoned, or another form of wasted, but he wasn't going to be fun to talk to. Convincing him to bless more water for me was going to be a debate, if not a full-on argument.

"I didn't recognize her. Is she new?" I asked, trying for the small talk angle.

"They all come to me eventually." He stood up and walked over to me. I was used to the routine. First he would flirt with me, a mock attempt at seduction that he had never and probably never would act on. He seemed to understand I was too disturbed by him to be attracted to him.

His oily black hair might have been shiny and beautiful if it were combed and trimmed. He was attractive with chiseled cheekbones and hollowed cheeks, but the five-going-on-eighty-day scruff was just too much to look past. Aside from the unhealthy gauntness he had achieved from choosing drugs over food, he had also developed a smell of alcohol that poured off of his breath and sweat.

He leaned into me, bracing his hands on the back of the pew. I leaned back and switched to breathing through my mouth instead of my nose. "They want answers. They want to know why God hates them. I have the answers, don't I, Lenore?"

It was cocaine. I could always tell his cocaine high from his marijuana high. Coke made him mean and hypersensitive. I wanted to fast-forward the process, and get to the end. I was tired of the speeches and the soapbox self-deprecation, but if I said the wrong thing, he wouldn't help me and I'd have to come back again. That was not on my wish-list.

He didn't wait for me to answer. He stood and gestured to the hanging crucifix behind the altar, which had become a coatrack for stray bras. "I have the answers because I am one of God's very own foot soldiers." He glanced back at me. "I committed my life to Him, you know? I gave up every vice for Him. How does he repay me?" Priest picked up a half-empty bottle of wine from the chancel steps and threw it at the crucifix. The glass missed the target and shattered wine onto the wall beside it. "He leaves me behind!"

Priest's voice echoed through the arched rafters of the church. It would have been dramatic except I had heard this speech before. The anger he exploited was no more than a childish fit to me now. As I said, I didn't begrudge him his emotions, but for him to think himself so much higher than the rest of us, that he should have the right to fall so far from his own predetermined grace, made him seem spoiled and arrogant. My sympathies for his situation, which was also my situation, had long since waned.

"You know what I have to say to that?" he seethed through bared teeth. "Fuck God!" He repeated it a few more times before rushing back to me. Desperately needing camaraderie in his rage, he clutched my shoulders and shook me fiercely. "Say it. Say it!"

"Fuck him."

"Louder!"

"Fuck him!" Although I could never bring myself to say "God" at the end of that blasphemy, he either didn't notice, or didn't care. It just felt wrong, even if it was an honest statement to come by at that point in my life.

Priest stared me down. His bloodshot green eyes danced over my face, never trespassing beyond my chin, despite his new hobby of lechery. He released me and knelt down before me, as if the entire scene had wasted his energies. "I'm sorry," he whispered before placing his head on my lap. I couldn't be sure if the apology was for me or for God, but it was something I had never heard before.

Not sure what to do to console him, I stroked his head. His hair was too long and in need of a good brushing, but it was silky—cleaner than I would have expected. After I had my fill of running my fingers through his hair, I tried to talk to him. Unfortunately, he had passed out.

I pushed him off me and gently lowered him back onto the cushioned pew where I had been sitting. He was going to be out for a while, I assumed, so I left without my holy water. I didn't want to repeat the visit, but Priest needed sleep more than I needed blessed water.

Sumo Training

"I DON'T UNDERSTAND WHY we're still doing this," I said as I slipped in a mouth guard. We were all outside the house in the front yard. Haden was openly tanning her slender legs on a blanket, while August was sitting in a plastic lawn chair outside the spray-painted circle Devin and I were standing in.

Devin had removed his shirt to get a little sun as well. I would have preferred it to be for my benefit, but his unveiling conveniently coincided with Haden's arrival. Yet another reminder of why I had said "no" to him several nights before. Why would I intentionally hurt myself?

"You need to get stronger. You need to learn to defend yourself," August chastised me with her motherly tone.

"Why? I have you," I insisted through my mouth guard.

"I won't always be there to save you." August adjusted the brim of her floppy beach hat. She wasn't as interested in the sun as the others were. Her toffee colored skin wasn't as fair as mine, but she still tended to burn rather than tan.

"Sure you will," I slurred over my appliance before smiling at her. She smiled back warmly before motioning for Devin to attack.

Devin dove into me. I did my best to stay in the circle, but he pushed me out right away. "Come on, Lenore. Aren't you even going to try?" Devin asked, disappointed.

"You weigh more than me. How am I supposed to stop you?"

"Don't stop him," Haden chimed in without looking over at us. "Just evade him." She sounded annoyed even though she was apparently trying to help.

"The point is to try," August said. "Don't give up when he starts pushing. Dig your feet in. Kick him. Punch him. Think of a child being kidnapped by a man. What should the child do to save himself?"

I ejected my slobber-covered mouth gear, a less than attractive moment for me. "It won't matter; he's stronger than me." August sighed before getting up and walking away. I looked to Devin for an explanation. "What does she want from me? I can't fight you."

"Yes, you can. You may not be able to win, but you can certainly fight. That's all she wants: just put up a good fight. The worst thing you can do is stand there and let yourself die."

I looked between August and him. They didn't understand me. My instincts said to run and hide. She was trying to make me a predator, but I was always going to be the prey. "I'm sorry, Devin. I can shoot an arrow, that's it. One misplaced checkmark for an archery class at summer camp. It doesn't make me a hunter and it certainly doesn't make me a warrior."

"Okay," Devin said, grinning at me mischievously.

"What?" I asked, narrowing my eyes.

"Defend yourself against this." Devin dove at me with tickling fingers. I squealed pathetically and squirmed from his grasp. I wasn't sure this was the type of defensive move August had in mind, but for the moment we seemed to be doing better than arguing.

I tried to get around behind him, but he grabbed me from behind and tickled my stomach. He had a knack for finding the most sensitive areas. I laughed until I coughed, but he didn't stop. Eventually I managed to trip him, but that only left him half on top of me, pinching the back of my thigh under my butt. I screamed and laughed, trying to buck him off.

"There you go." He laughed at me. "There is a little fight in you." I got my hand free and slapped his face, but as soon as I did it, I gasped and apologized. He pinched me harder. "Stop apologizing. I've been slapped harder than that before."

His hand shifted between my legs slipping under the hem of my shorts. I grabbed his hand to stop him from going any further. My laughter died, and he smirked at me. A question passed over his face, but he never asked it. He pinched my skin on my inner thigh, before withdrawing his attack.

He rolled off me and we both got back to our feet. Haden's attention had been drawn to the display, and she was already getting up to interrupt us if we didn't stop on our own. "Let me show you how it's done," she said, stepping into the circle and waving me off.

I stepped outside the line and stupidly expected to learn something from watching them. The only thing I learned was that Haden didn't want to share Devin with me. They danced around a bit before the pushing and shoving resulted in Devin landing on top of Haden.

The so-called sweet talk they shared, as they not so discreetly shifted to better match their bodies, was enough to make a sailor blush. It was more than enough to send me away.

August had wandered back to the house. I found her sitting on the stoop watching the action from a distance. She shook her head when I approached. "I'm sorry, August," I said. "I'm not cut out to fight. I wish you wouldn't waste your time. I hate disappointing you over and over again."

She nodded over to the circle where Haden and Devin were openly making out. "Why do you let her walk all over you like that?"

"Cause she can kick my ass." I crossed my arms and kicked the cement step beside her.

"I can see you like Devin. There is no reason to deny yourself a little companionship." I nodded even though this conversation felt like a sex talk with my mother. "Devin is a good man. He will be respectful and discreet."

"Haden and him—"

"—are chaotic," she finished. "But that has nothing to do with you. Haden doesn't own Devin. Don't let her dictate your level of celibacy. If you won't fight to save your life, at least fight for the little pleasures in your life."

I grunted some kind of nonspecific response. "I would fight to save my life. I'm not completely suicidal. But it's hard to motivate myself to fight my friends. For real, I mean. I can't bring myself to scratch out Devin's eyes, you know?"

August nodded thoughtfully at me. "I understand," she said distantly, as if a plot was forming in her mind. Knowing her it probably was. Since she was usually pretty creative, I was sure I wasn't going to like it.

Strawberries

AUGUST'S STATEMENT ABOUT CELIBACY reminded me I still needed to get holy water from Priest, so I took the truck back out to his church. The trip wasn't far, but it was nice to get away from the house. No matter how lonely you get in life, you can still appreciate some privacy.

Alone in the truck, I blared Jimmy the Card's radio broadcast. He usually played upbeat music during the day hours. In the weekday evenings, he switched to soft rock, but the weekend nights, he played heavy dance and rap music.

There were always parties on the weekends. In the rural areas, we went to barn dances—literally in barns on someone's farm. Jimmy would announce the invitations to his listeners and we went to whichever was the closest. The parties usually consist of dancing, drinking, and finding someone to take a roll in the hay with—again literally.

Past the witching hour Jimmy switched to romantic melodies to cater to the couples spending the night in each other's arms. I was usually passed out long before that, but I was told if you made it to three a.m. Jimmy put on a pornographic recitation for all of his female fans who preferred to spend their nights with him. Essentially, live broadcasted phone sex. What the hell, the FCC was no longer functional.

After a lot of off-key singing, I arrived at the church for another round of Priest's anti-God rhetoric. As usual, I listened at the door to make sure I didn't walk in on anything. Given my last visit, it wasn't a foolproof method, but calling ahead wasn't an option, since the church didn't have a phone, and Priest rarely went back to his rectory.

As I listened at the door, I heard a few pleasure-summoned moans from women inside. I cursed my luck and walked around to the garden instead of retreating back to the truck. I knew from experience this might be a long wait, but I didn't want to make the trip again tomorrow.

August and the others didn't trust Priest—with good reason. People high on coke and other drugs tended to do bad things. They objected to my visits, whether they were necessary or not. Twice in one week was already causing second and third glances between them. I wasn't sure if they were afraid Priest was going to hurt me, or just influence me to his side of madness.

The apocalypse had brought about a plague of unmowed lawns, but Priest had managed to keep his garden in functioning order, which was strange, since he didn't keep himself in functioning order. To my surprise and glee, I found a patch of strawberries that were ripe for the picking.

I sat down and started picking. Without regard to the red juice spilling down my chin and fingers, I relished the little berries. I'm pretty sure I may have eaten a bug or two as well, but that was no matter when the little bits of fruit were so sweet.

"What the hell do you think you are doing?" Priest's voice bellowed, shattering my epicurean thoughts.

I looked up and found him standing over me with his hands on his hips. The sun blocked my view of his face, so I couldn't tell how mad he was. I blinked against the light and spat out the top of my strawberry. "I was just tasting a few."

"Tasting? Is that what you call this piggery display?" He threw out his hand and I flinched, fearing the worst. "Come with me. I'll show you how to eat strawberries."

I put my hand in his and he pulled me up, tugging me back into the church. When I dragged behind him instead of walking beside him, he switched his grip from my hand to around my shoulders. I was used to him being proximately drunk, but the cozy guided tour up his church aisle was out of character. The fact I couldn't smell alcohol on him was even more unusual.

The moans I heard from before were still coming from two women on the steps in front of the altar. They were sharing strawberries, Lady and the Tramp style. After each bite they kissed and moaned with enjoyment.

"I don't want to eat my strawberries like that," I said as I added a little more drag to my step.

Priest chuckled. "They're both high on acid. They could be sharing day-old French fries and they would still think it was the most wonderful food they ever ate."

"Are you on acid?" I asked without thinking.

He stopped and pulled away from me. He looked at me, and for the first time I looked at him. He seemed well rested without the usual sagging eyelids and bloodshot eyes of a pothead. His face had regained some fullness like he had remembered to eat. "No."

"Why not?" I asked, simultaneously wondering when I had taken the muzzle off my mouth.

"I thought I could use a break," he said and ushered me forward into the front pew. "You came to see me a couple days ago, didn't you?" he asked before moving to the altar to pick up an extra bowl of washed and hulled strawberries.

"You remember that?" I said sarcastically. My mouth was on a roll.

"Barely," he admitted. He returned to the pew and sat next to me. "I remember the look on your face."

"What was it this time? Fear, anger, pity—?"

"Disgust," he said flatly, before I could rattle off the remaining emotions I usually felt around him. That wasn't one I would have admitted to, but it was definitely on the list. "I disgust you, don't I?"

I wasn't sure why that surprised him. He was a drugged-up, orgy-having, former priest. What wasn't disgusting about that? Perhaps he assumed his actions were so piteous it was beyond that level of reproach. Or maybe he just finally saw the depth of my disgust.

I shrugged and looked away. His hand pulled my chin back so swiftly I brought my hands up to defend myself. His fingers clutched my chin, while I dug my fingernails into his wrist. He either didn't feel it, or didn't care. "Tell me what you really feel. I'm sober now. Sober enough to hear it, anyway."

"Get your hand off me," I said. He released my chin, but I kept my hand around his wrist until he relaxed back into the pew. "What do you want to know, Priest?"

"Why do you still call me that?" he mumbled.

"Why do you still wear your collar, when you are clearly no longer holy?"

"Because I'm mad at God."

"And no one else is?" I asked. "Do you seriously think you are the only one who is dumbfounded by this whole thing?"

"I shouldn't be here!" His voice boomed, but he didn't move.

"Are you sure about that?" I yelled back. He was sober so I had no need to tiptoe over his addle-brained temperament. "Look at you." I pushed away from the pew to get a view of him. "You are apocalyptic roadkill. You devoted your whole life to God, and when things didn't go the way you thought they should, you not only released yourself from your obligations, you practically signed your soul over to Lucifer instead."

I stood up to face him. "Maybe he left you behind because he knew you were weak and would break like a Fabergé egg." Priest started to object to that statement, but I put up a hand to stop him. "You thought you saw disgust in my eyes. Well, you did, but not for the reason you think." His urgency to interrupt waned, and he started to listen again. "You think I'm disgusted because you are a drunken, lecherous drug addict who wallows in his own self-pity, but that's not what disgusts me. What disgusts me is that you are all of those things, and you *still* think you're better than the rest of us!"

I didn't wait for a response. I headed to the door. I had said my piece, which was more than I ever expected to be able to say. Even if I had remembered I needed holy water I wouldn't have cared.

Priest had caught up with me at the doors and interposed himself between me and my exit. "Wait," he said, with pleading eyes. "You're right." He put his hands up to touch me, but didn't actually make contact. "Please don't leave." I must have looked as confused as I felt. I had just told him he was a selfish, egotistical, fuck-up, so why did he want me to stay? "You need more holy water, don't you?"

"I can get it another day." I made a move to the door, even though I had no hope he would move.

"Another day I may not be sober," he said, finally grasping my hands. "Please, Lenore, I sobered up just to talk to you. I wanted to hear you without the clutter of my crutches. I don't know if I'll be sober tomorrow. Stay with me today while I am."

"Why?" I looked him over for the trap.

"Because my harem—as you call them—are not good conversationalists when I'm not as high as they are." I glanced back at the two women who would be content for hours with their strawberry kisses. When I turned back to offer an excuse or a stipulation, Priest squeezed my hands hard. "You are the only sober friend I have left in my life, Lenore."

I had never thought of myself as his friend before, but that was probably because I didn't think he thought of me as a friend. I could always use more friends. "You do realize you're just using me as a crutch to avoid your other crutches?"

"Yes, but it doesn't mean I don't want you here as much as I need you."

"I'll stay, but not in here." I motioned back to the women. "You need to get some sun anyway."

Sunshine and Other Natural Remedies

PRIEST TOOK IN A deep breath as we sat looking over the pond behind his gardens. The silence must have been relaxing to him, but to me it was uncomfortable. He brought the strawberries with him, but hadn't offered them, so I was still waiting for snack time. The blanket we were lounging on was a tattered quilt that looked like it had a story. The smell indicated it was an old story.

"I love this place," he said eventually. "I used to fish back here. I probably still could, if I could manage to stay sober."

"You need to get the hell out of here, Priest." I leaned back on the blanket to absorb the sun's warmth.

"What? Why?"

"You're like a divorced couple who insists on living together, when you clearly hate each other. You and God might be broken up, but it doesn't mean you should hang out and continuously hurt each other. Just walk away. Let the festering pain of loss be healed by time and distance. Get a dog or something."

Priest laughed. It was the first time it didn't sound maniacal to me. "A dog instead of God, is that supposed to be meaningful?"

"No, I just like dogs."

"You have an interesting logic, Lenore." He leaned back on the blanket as well, resting on his side, facing me. "Honest, but simple." I shrugged in response. I wasn't sure if simple logic made me simple-minded, but I was sure it was meant as a compliment. "What about you? How are things going with your foursome?"

"We aren't a foursome. We are a group of friends."

"You're polygamists."

"Is that judgment I hear?" I tipped my head as if to better hear his answer.

"No," Priest quickly corrected.

"Life is too lonely. Taboos don't matter right now. Besides, I'm not sleeping with Devin."

"You're not?" he asked incredulously.

"Why does that sound so strange to everyone?"

"Because I've seen how you look at him: puppy crush and then some."

"I guess I'm more of a monogamist than I thought."

"There's nothing wrong with that. Sometimes we want what we want. Speaking of want, do you want the strawberries now?"

"It's about time," I said, reaching for the bowl as he brought it over.

"Uh-uh-uh," he said, pulling the bowl out of my grasp. "I still have to show you how to eat them."

"Open, insert, chew, chew, just gimme." I reached out my palm for an offering.

"Close your eyes," he said softly.

"What? No way, I'm not doing anything kinky."

He grimaced at that. "Have I ever acted inappropriately toward you?" he asked earnestly. I shook my head. "Have I ever hurt you?" I shook my head again, starting to feel sheepish. "Why would my being sober change that?"

I didn't bother answering. I just settled into the blanket and closed my eyes. I still didn't trust him and flinched when I felt his hand move across my body to place the bowl. "Relax, Lenore," he drawled. "I promise this isn't sexual, it's just savoring life."

When he asked me to open my mouth and I opened like a fish out of water, he laughed at me. "Not so big, just... forgive the description, but... pretend you're about to kiss someone. Part your lips to receive it."

Instinctively, I licked my lips and opened slightly. When I felt the strawberry touch my lips, I tipped my chin to eat it, but he pulled it away. "Not so fast. See why you have to be taught? Food is about more than taste. Trust me, I used to be celibate, I know how to enjoy a meal."

I laughed at that and parted my lips again. Priest dragged the bitten strawberry across my lips. It was cool, sweet, and despite Priest's intentions it felt innately sexual to me. "Lick your lips." I did so, enjoying the distinct taste only strawberries could provide. "Open." I opened and he rested the strawberry in my mouth. "Chew slowly, like it's the last food you will ever eat."

I chewed slowly, only swallowing when my saliva threatened to choke me. Priest repeated the procedure again, offering me a smell of the berry first. When we were on our fifth berry I not only felt full, I felt like I no longer cared if Priest's intentions were honorable. Somewhere between taste and touch, I had lost track of what I was supposed to be getting out of this experience.

"What's going on here?" August's voice called from above us.

I sat up even before opening my eyes. I hit Priest in the forehead on my ascent, which ushered him back, hissing in pain.

"August?" I said, blinking away the sun. "What are you doing here?" She was standing over us, eyeballing the blanket and the strawberries.

"You've been gone two hours. How long does it take to get holy water?" She looked mad, like she had caught me making out with my boyfriend on the couch.

"I didn't realize I was expected back at a certain time. I could have taken the four-wheeler or the bike."

"Never mind that, what's going on here?"

Before I could answer, Priest stood up. "What does it matter, August? We're eating strawberries. I asked her to stay. She is my friend."

"I don't want you influencing her, Matthew. I need her sober."

"Strawberries, August." Priest pointed to the bowl. "Not cocaine."

"Lenore, get your holy water and get the truck back home. I don't want you hanging out here all day."

"I'm not going to start using drugs because of him," I defended myself.

"No, I'm not worried about that. What I am worried about is your hope getting caught up in..." August twirled her finger over the scene. "...this. He won't stay sober for long, Lenore."

I looked up at Priest. He didn't offer any objection to this. "I know," I said, somewhat forlorn. "Let me enjoy it while I can." She looked a little put off by the comment, but she nodded and left us without another word.

Priest shuffled about angrily before sitting back down on the blanket. "I'm sorry," he said.

"For what? She's my friend. I should be apologizing to you."

"No, I'm sorry she's right. Addict or not, I don't want to be sober in this world anymore."

"I never expected you to sober up for me. I didn't even know we were friends until today." He looked hurt by that; I grimaced apologetically. "I know now." He smiled and reached over to touch my cheek. He closed his eyes and whispered something that sounded Latin. When he opened his eyes, he looked sad. "What did you just do?"

"I blessed you, and asked God to protect you."

"You guys are on speaking terms now?"

"I never stopped talking to God," he said flatly. "He just stopped answering." He winked at me, to let me know he wasn't intending to sound crazy. "I should get you your water, so you can get out of here."

"I'm not in a rush." I handed him the flask from my back pocket so he could bless the water it contained. "After that display I'm obligated to stay longer just to flaunt my independence."

"August didn't come here to get you to come home. She came here to tell me I'm not good enough for you." He closed his eyes and blessed the flask. When he opened his eyes, he was looking directly at me. "She's right."

I sat up further on the blanket. I didn't know how to react to this. Until now I didn't know I was friends with Priest, and now that I did, he was essentially telling me we couldn't be friends. "Priest—" It was all I got out before he handed me the flask.

"I'm sorry, Lenore. I wish I could be more than selfish, but right now, all I have left in this world is arguing with my ex." With that Priest stalked off to do who knows what sin. I didn't follow.

Fires Within

I T WAS HARD FOR me to be mad at August. It was hard for me to be mad at anyone I loved, because I hated conflict, but it was especially hard with her. She was like my mother, sister, and best friend all rolled into one and I couldn't bring myself to defy her or fight with her, even if I did think her opinion of Priest was shortsighted.

She was right about one thing: Priest was not going to sober up because I told him he should. But she was wrong that I was going to get hurt by him. She thought I was expecting him to go back to the way he was before the apocalypse. I had no hope of that. All I wanted was for him to stop wallowing in misery. If he wanted to drink and smoke pot, then at least let it be for pleasure, not numbing.

I managed to stay out of everyone's way until the weekend was over. We went to a few parties that ended the same way they always did. I went home early on the four-wheeler to snooze, while everyone else hung around to schmooze. As usual, the early night shift lacked any major glimmer grim, at least nothing I couldn't simply drive around to get away from.

When I got home early for what had to be the eighth week in a row, I made a decision. I was going to sleep with Devin. It shouldn't have received the cresting excitement I felt, but I wasn't going to sleep with him for reasons of love or even lust. I was going to sleep with him because I was mad.

I'm not sure how being mad meant I should sleep with Devin, but in my head it made sense. I was going to piss off Haden, but I didn't care. I was sick of being a prude through the apocalypse while everyone else was living it up.

Truthfully, I think what I wanted to do was sleep with Priest to piss August off, but as I said before, it's hard for me to be mad at her. To outright go against her wasn't going to work. However, sleeping with someone she approved of, while pretending it was someone she didn't approve of, might offer me the revenge I desired, without the repercussions.

Yes, that actually sounded logical in my head.

Monday night was fairly boring, or it would have been had my decision to sleep with Devin not encouraged a good number of stupid follow-up decisions.

First, there was the liquid courage. I certainly couldn't just tell Devin I wanted to sleep with him. Because I was a coward, but also because it would be anticlimactic. After all, he had been waiting a long time for me to give in to my desires.

The second stupid decision was the dress. I didn't have a lot of sexy clothes, so I altered a long dress from my closet to make it a short dress. It was a little too short, and after I removed the sleeves and cut into the bodice to add lace, it was much too revealing. It was a few pounds too tight as well. When I finally slipped it on, my breasts were mashed so tight, I looked like I was wearing a corset.

My third stupid decision was making my intentions known to Devin in front of everyone. Alas, all the other decisions prior to that could have been expunged if I had only discreetly dragged Devin upstairs for a private rendezvous.

By the time, I made it down to the bonfire in the backyard, I was thoroughly toasted. My three friends were illuminated by the fire they were sitting around. When I arrived, August started speaking before the firelight had illuminated me.

"Oh, Lenore, at last, I want you to..." She trailed off as the fire revealed my *very* little black dress. "What are you wearing?"

"I wanted something nice to mark the occasion," I said—or slurred, depending on how it sounded to them.

Devin whistled. "Well, well, well, Lenore. I wasn't sure you had any shape under those t-shirts, but there you are."

"Shut up, Devin," Haden snarled.

"It's okay, Haden," I said, misinterpreting the reason for her defensiveness. "I don't mind the attention. Not tonight." I sat down on Devin's lap and he jumped in shock, but welcomed me by wrapping his arms around my waist.

"What has gotten into you, Lenore?" August chided.

"Nothing... yet." I smiled and squirmed against Devin's lap. He smiled broadly and chuckled.

"Are you drunk?" August asked, standing up.

"Yeah, yeah, shush mom." I waved my hand and leaned in to kiss Devin. He pulled away, but didn't stop smiling.

"I can't do that while you're drunk, girl." He shook his head.

"It's the only way I can," I whispered and bit his earlobe, since he couldn't pull any farther away. He moaned and urged me closer despite his reservations to my inebriated state.

"Devin!" The snap sounded from both August and Haden.

"Okay!" he said, pulling me away. "Oh, sweet thing, why couldn't you have done this last night, or any other night before this night."

"What's wrong?" I asked, running my hand up his leg. He made no attempts to stop me until August ground out his name again. He pulled my hand to his lips and kissed it. All the while his eyes sparkled with delight.

"I'm going to have to ask you not to do that," he said, "but for the record, yes, yes, and yes."

I smiled and slipped out of his lap. There was a lot more opposition to our hook-up than I thought there would be, but I was determined to get Devin on my side. "What do I have to do to convince you?" I asked.

To add to my already egregious humiliation, I started to dance: a slither in my body, a roll in my shoulders, and a dip in my knees. It might have looked more like an epileptic seizure though.

"This is not the time or place for this, Lenore." August moved to stop me, but Devin grabbed her and pulled her down to his lap.

"No, no, no, this is too priceless to interrupt. You go girl!"

"Don't encourage her," August said, struggling against his grip.

"Oh, let her have her moment," he said. "Lord knows you aren't going to let her have anything else before she goes."

"Goes?" I asked in the middle of a crouched shimmy. "Where am I going?" I stood up without consideration for my center of gravity, my blood alcohol level, or the fire behind me. I faltered and fell right at the hot blaze.

I could see August struggling to get off Devin in time to save me, but for the first time ever, I realized she was right. She couldn't be there to save me every time. I pinched my eyes and waited to feel the burn. I only hoped I could get out before my hair caught on fire.

I never hit the coals. Arms braced my back and scooped me away from the growing heat. When I opened my eyes, I saw the man holding me. A strange man.

I didn't wait for introductions. I screamed and punched him in the face. He dropped me and I crawled to the safety of August's legs.

"Lenore," August said, "I'd like you to meet my brother, Garrett."

Sisters?

"WHAT THE HELL WERE you thinking?" Haden dragged me into the house by my wrist. She might have preferred to be dragging me in by my ear, but she wouldn't have gotten me very far, since I was still too drunk to function without a sober-eye-dog.

"I wanted to get back at her," I said as I stumbled up the stairs after her and into my bedroom.

"For what?"

"She thinks I can't be friends with Priest, without getting hurt."

"What?" Haden pushed me down on my bed. Perfectly content with my flopped position, I watched her search my closet for non-whore clothing. "She just doesn't like him. None of us do. He's a freaking priest who didn't get taken at the reckoning. Imagine what he must have done to deserve that."

"He's not bad! He's just broken!" I yelled much louder than necessary.

"Shut... up." Haden clamped her fingers together, indicating how my mouth should be. I should have said *"fuck you,"* but the alcohol decided crying was a much more scathing riposte. "Oh, for crap's sake, Lenore, you are so bad at drinking."

She knelt down before me and pulled off my high heels before removing my dress. "I'm sorry, Haden," I whined. She glanced up before pulling me to stand. "I shouldn't have tried to sleep with Devin. I know how much you love him."

"Love...? What...?" She sighed. "Is that why you never went for him? Cause you thought I would be mad?"

I nodded and sniffled. "Wouldn't you be?"

"Hell yes, but no madder than if you ate my chips. I hate to share."

I shook my head. "You two can pretend all you want, but I see how much you want each other."

Haden grabbed an extra big wad of tissues from my bedside table and shoved it to my nose. "Blow." I blew and she viciously pinched away what must have been assaulting her view. "Look, you do whatever you want with Devin. I might be mad, but I'll get over it. This is the end of days. I've got no reason to hold a grudge, especially against one of my sisters."

"Sisters?" I asked.

"Yeah, stupid, what did you think we were?"

"I thought you hated me," I said.

"No," she snarled. "I don't hate you. I like you, but you do annoy the crap out of me, so yeah, that makes us sisters, right?"

I hugged her. I wasn't sure it was the alcohol either. She had never expressed anything but irritation toward me. I was relieved she didn't hate me. She returned the embrace for a moment, and aside from my partial nudity, and my nose threatening to leak on her shirt, it was nice.

After she pushed me away, she proceeded to dress me like a child: pulling my pants up for me, and slipping my arms into my shirt. I buttoned my pants and tucked in the shirt. She pressed on my back to usher me back downstairs, but I hugged her instead. She tried to pull away, but I tightened my grip, and she gave in. I thanked her and released her.

The second hug was definitely the alcohol.

We came downstairs and found the party had moved into the kitchen, so we joined everyone there. My approach slowed as I sensed the *family meeting* ambiance. Haden jerked my wrist and nodded her head up at me, indicating I should keep my chin up or be brave, or some such inspirational bullshit.

"Hellooo sexy," Devin drawled shortly before Haden punched him in the gut on the way by. It must have hurt because he didn't say anything more. Haden sat down at the table with Garrett and August. Devin was standing, leaving one open chair available opposite Garrett.

"Sit down, Lenore," August instructed.

I glanced at Devin, hoping he might be able to take the seat in my stead. Despite looking a little green from his gut punch, he smiled and mouthed, "It's okay." I took the seat, keeping myself a good foot from the table. The kitchen felt small with five people in it and my claustrophobia was rearing its head.

"Lenore Evans, this is my half-brother Garrett Smith," August repeated the introduction, but this time, instead of being quickly ushered off with Haden, I shook his hand. Garrett was a rusty blond with buzz-cut hair, and hard muscular features. His square chin was only slightly overshadowed by his nose, which was a little too big, but he was attractive. Not as attractive as Devin, but really, who was?

"Nice to meet you," I said. I was still pretty drunk, but I was not without my sense of embarrassment for my earlier display. He no doubt saw most of it from the shadows beyond the firelight. If he was in any way amused by me, he didn't show it—just the opposite. He looked bored, like he realized his blind date was a taxidermist, and he still had three more meal courses to go before he could graciously leave. "I didn't know you had a brother," I told August.

"You will be leaving with Garrett tonight," August stated as if the entire conversation leading up to that decision had already happened, including the explanation for this nomadic conclusion.

"Say what?" I looked at Garrett. He wasn't surprised by the statement. He barely looked at me. He seemed to have found a fleck of dried noodle on the table and was determined to scratch it off.

"Garrett is going to train you in self-defense," August said matter-of-factly.

"Oh, geez, not this again." I stood up, but Devin blocked my escape. I must have looked as betrayed as I felt because he looked sheepish.

"Please, sit and listen," he whispered before squeezing my shoulder. Had it not been him, I might have been gruffly pushed into my chair. As it was, when I finally sat, he made it a point to rub my shoulders to keep me down. My claustrophobia flared again.

"I need you to be part of this group," August said. "In order to do that, you need to train. You said yourself, you can't fight us. You know us all too well. I'm confident my brother can train you to be who you need to be."

"Who *you* want me to be?" I said snidely.

"I'm not asking you to change yourself into someone new. I'm asking you to become the woman you are supposed to become."

"I am who I'm supposed to be," I said. "I'm fine with who I am."

Garrett looked at August. "I see what you mean." As I suspected his voice was deep, and the hard edge to his tone confirmed he didn't just *look* like an asshole.

"What did she mean?" I stared down Garrett and crossed my arms for effect. I tried to shrug away Devin's hands, but he was no longer hiding the fact he was holding me down. "What did she say about me?"

Garrett looked me over like he was making his own assessment. "That you're stubborn. However, I disagree. I think you're lazy."

"Excuse me! You don't even know me, dirtbag!"

"Big words for someone who can't back them up." Garrett leaned back in his chair.

"Did she tell you I can hit a grim in the eye from a hundred feet?" I bragged.

"Is that supposed to impress me? What can you hit at two feet?" Garrett leaned forward over the table. "How about now? I'm a grim sitting at your table. You got in a lucky shot outside; let's see if you can do it again."

"You wouldn't make it that close to me if I had my bow and arrow," I said.

"That's the point, Lenore." August was no longer making any effort to hide her exasperation. "He *was* that close to you outside. He was just outside of the firelight, and you never saw him. You never even suspected someone was there."

"I was drunk," I said.

"Would it have mattered?" August asked. "You assume we will take care of it. You never even worry. You're a liability to us, and until you can be more than my cook, you can't stay here."

I struggled against Devin, before I slipped out of his grasp and away from the table. "Get off me! Fuck you! Fuck all of you!"

I ran upstairs, away from them all. I secured myself behind my locked door and fell into my bed. Seconds later there was a knock on my door.

"Lenore." August's voice sounded soft, but I knew she was frustrated with me. I didn't have much sympathy since I was pissed at her. "Open the—"

Before she could finish the frame splintered around the door as Garrett kicked it in. I yelped and jumped up, using my bed as a barrier between me and my invaders.

"Was that really necessary?" August pushed past him to get inside.

"Leave me alone!" I sounded like a teenager screaming at my parents, but I didn't care.

"Just knock her out," Garrett grumbled.

I gaped at him. I knew August wanted me to defend myself, but was she seriously considering handing me over to this ape in order to get it?

"No," August scolded, "she goes voluntarily, or there'll be nothing more to discuss." She stopped at the foot of my bed to speak to me. "Lenore, please don't make me force this on you. You have to learn to identify trouble. You can't always depend on a weapon that will eventually run out of ammunition. Why do you think I don't carry a gun?"

I glanced at Garrett, who was eyeing me like a hawk. I couldn't stand the idea of going anywhere with him. "How can you ask me to leave you?" My voice started to shake with the pain I felt from this potential abandonment. "I love you," I whispered, trying to stay below the squawk of emotion forming in my throat.

August frowned and she approached me with the motherly warmth I wanted and needed at that moment. "I'm not asking you to leave. I'm asking you to make yourself strong and then come back to me."

I shook my head. "I don't want to be strong. I want things to stay the way they are. I don't want to lose anyone else. I don't want to be alone again."

August closed the distance between us and hugged me. She stroked my hair as I leaned into her. I could tell she was soundlessly arguing with Garrett over my shoulder. "If I let you stay here, will you promise to let him train you?" she asked. My heart leapt with relief and I nodded into her shoulder. "No matter what, you have to do as he asks. You have to listen to his instruction as if he were me."

"I don't like him," I whispered even though he could probably hear me.

"I don't need you to like him. It will be easier to fight him if you don't, remember?"

I drew back and looked at her. "You brought him here so I had someone to fight. Someone I won't feel bad about hurting."

"That's essentially the gist of it," she said.

I looked back at Garrett. He was standing at the door, looking as perturbed by this whole scene as that blind date he was just on. "I don't think I'll feel bad about hurting him."

Home Sweet Home

A TTENTION TO DETAIL WAS never my strong suit. When August suggested I could stay at the house to train, I never imagined it meant her, Devin, and Haden would leave me behind with no vehicles and an arrogant prick for a trainer.

I stared out at the empty driveway. I hadn't heard the engines start, but sometime last night they had left to stock up groceries and left again with their travel bags. They weren't planning on returning any time soon. A week, a month... I hoped not more than a month. I was mad, but I had made my promise, so I started doing whatever Garrett asked, as if he were August.

He started me out on basic calisthenics and running. If all else failed, he would have me ready to outrun a mature grim in no time. We started swordplay, which was kind of fun, except when I stumbled he would thwack me with the side of his blade until I got back up. It was the type of negative reinforcement I didn't respond to well.

After two weeks, I came to realize this was not going to be just a month of training. I was disappointed, but I didn't have time to gripe about it, since every day was packed full of training exercises. The only conversation Garrett and I had was instructional, or necessary. *Do you want gravy?*—wasn't exactly what I called small talk.

Still, I endured everything he shoved at me, including the ridiculous wrestling moves I recognized from high school competitions. It wasn't until the beginning of week three I got to try out some actual self-defense moves, and that was only because I literally had to defend myself.

"Dinner will be done in a few minutes," I said as Garrett came into the kitchen. I expected the comment would be met with the same wordless grunt it usually was, but instead he pulled me away from the stove with a thick arm around my waist and bent me face first over the table.

I screamed or cursed or something, but it all blurred into shock and fear. He grabbed my hair and pulled my head back. His other hand was down my shirt, gripping my breast. "I need an appetizer," he said and I could smell the alcohol on his breath.

I kicked and screamed, but he slammed my head into the table and started undoing my pants. I leaned onto the table further and used both my feet to kick the inside of his knee. He yelled and stumbled back in pain, freeing me to escape.

I ran for the back door, but he tackled me. He pressed a chef's knife to my throat—he had grabbed it from my wood block. I shoved his hand away and pushed myself up to crawl from underneath him. He hooked his finger in the belt loop on my jeans and flipped me over. He pressed the tip of the blade sharply into my throat. "Undo your pants, or I'll slice you open and finish with your corpse."

There might have been more to that sentence, but I punched him in his Adam's apple. He withdrew the knife, unable to resist clasping his hands on his aching throat. I thought I would be able to get away, but he punched me in the face. The blinding pain paralyzed me for a moment. It took me a second to realize the tongue in my mouth was not my own.

Garrett was on top of me, pushing his lips onto mine. I bit his tongue and he pulled away. He slapped me, but I ignored the pain. I pushed his knife-wielding hand into his *still cocked* slapping hand, forcing him to gouge his own flesh. He must have been surprised, because I was still able to punch his crotch and upper-cut his chin before he had a chance to slash me with the knife.

My forearm bled heavily from the retaliation, but I wasn't concerned. I pushed the knife up again. As I suspected, he overcompensated to push against me so I didn't cut him again. I turned his wrist as he pushed back. The knife embedded firmly in the linoleum beside me. He pulled back on it, but it slipped from his grip.

I grabbed the blade prepared for the extra tug it would take to release it. He jumped off me to avoid my newly acquired weapon, and I threw it at his head. It was intended to be my shining moment in the battle, but the hilt hit his shoulder impotently, shattering any hopes I might have had about joining the circus.

Luckily, I was an ever-devoted scaredy-cat and already had my exit strategy in motion. I was up and opening the door before the knife hit the floor. I slipped out just as he started to charge after me.

I hadn't planned what to do when I got outside, but I did what I do best. I ran. As an afterthought, I realized what I needed to do. There was only one person left in my life to run to.

The Great Escape

W HEN I ARRIVED, I was wet with sweat, wet with tears, and wet with blood. I couldn't imagine what Priest thought when I burst through his church doors. "Priest!" I stumbled down the aisle, trying to find a happy medium between crying and breathing.

He was standing at the altar with one of his female friends. I was relieved that whatever they were about to do hadn't started yet. "Lenore?" He scrambled around the altar fully robed in what probably would have been saved for an Easter ceremony. It didn't matter.

Priest reached me in four long running strides. He caught hold of me and lifted me into his arms before he could see my injuries weren't *that* serious. "What the hell happened to you?"

"I didn't know where else to go. He tried to rape me."

"Who tried to rape you?" he asked, enraged by even the *tried* part.

"I did," Garrett's voice sounded at the door. My head whipped around, and between me wanting to run again, and Priest wanting to attack him, I was out of his arms in one swift movement.

"You followed me?" I asked behind Priest's arm. I wasn't sure if he was pressing me behind him, or if I was cowering there, but I was content to grip onto his arm like it was a life preserver.

"Technically, I arrived before you. I still have my motorcycle, remember? I knew exactly where you were going. August told me about your... friend."

"She didn't mention you." Priest took a step forward I wasn't ready to take, so it looked as if I was holding him back. "Who are you, and what did you do to Lenore?"

"My name is Garrett, I'm August's brother. She brought me here to train Lenore. Until tonight, I haven't really been training her so much as preparing her. Tonight, I attacked her."

"You tried to rape me!" I screamed at him and took that step forward I didn't want to take before. However, I was still firmly plastered to Priest's arm, so it didn't look especially threatening.

Garrett looked down at the floor before answering. "Yes, that is what I appeared to be doing. I would not have done that, but I needed you to believe I was going to do something to you. I needed you to be afraid enough to fight. You did well, by the way."

"Fuck you! I hate you!"

"That's okay," he said, returning his gaze to Priest. "Could we speak alone, Matthew, as gentlemen?" Garrett held up his hands in surrender.

After a long moment of evaluation on Priest's part, he nodded. "One moment." Priest turned around, pulling his right arm from my grasp in exchange for his left arm around my back. "Come with me."

"Priest, no. Don't talk to him. Just tell him to leave," I begged as we headed to the front of the church.

He shushed me gently as he led me into his dressing room off the side of the sanctuary. After he closed the door behind us, he slipped off his vestments and hung them up carefully. The casual jeans and t-shirt he had underneath were something I had never seen on him. Without the robe and collar, he looked almost normal—whatever that was at this point.

There was a small bathroom within the room, basically a closet with a toilet and sink. We both squished into it and he set me on the toilet while he washed the blood off my arm. I watched him fiddle in his first aid kit before he found the butterfly bandages he wanted.

He glanced at me before he started. His eyes were a little red, but he seemed lucid enough to trust with my care. He smiled at my no doubt stupefied expression. I couldn't understand why he treated me with such reverence, while he played with the insecurities of other women to get them into his bed, or in this case, onto his altar.

"Did you know I wanted to be a doctor?" he said as he kneeled down in front of me. I shook my head. "Before I wanted to be a priest, I wanted to help people, save lives, all that jazz." He pulled my cut together and placed the butterfly bandages. "I decided I could save people in a different way." He brought out a gauze roll and wrapped it around my forearm. I was mesmerized by the unraveling fabric. "Maybe I should have stuck with being a doctor."

Before he finished, I leaned forward and kissed his forehead as a thank you. I probably would have kissed his lips, but his forehead was much more accessible. "You're doing a pretty good job tonight, either way," I said. He smiled and placed his hand on my cheek. He mumbled a blessing before opening his eyes. "Why do you keep blessing me?"

"Because you don't know how insane it is to seek me out to save you from a lecherous man."

"You're not a rapist," I argued.

"No, I'm worse." He squeezed my shoulder before dropping his hand entirely out of contact. "I'm a seducer."

"You're going to let him take me back, aren't you?"

"Is he really training you?" he asked, rather than answer me.

"Yes," I whispered. "August and the others left so I could work on my self-defense skills with Garrett.

"Do you think what he said was true? Was he just pretending to rape you?"

The sudden attack did seem out of character for Garrett. He barely paid any attention to me, let alone demonstrate any attraction to me. "Maybe, but he was pretty convincing as a rapist."

"I'll talk to him, but to answer your question: no, I'm not letting anyone take you. I will, however, let you leave if we can trust what he says." He pulled me up and walked me back to the door. "There is a vent in the bottom of the door, so you'll be able to hear us." He frowned and touched my cheek where Garrett had punched me. His jaw clenched, but he didn't say anything before he slipped out the door.

Man to Man

THROUGH THE VENT, I could see and hear everything, especially since Priest forced Garrett to come forward by sitting on the steps of the chancel. Garrett sauntered up cautiously, while Priest lounged his elbows comfortably on the step behind him. "How much did August tell you about me?" Priest asked.

"She told me of your many vices. She also told me Lenore trusts you and that she would go to you if she thought she needed help."

"Yeah." Priest chuckled. "I can't break her of that little habit. What about tonight? You expect me to believe you were only *pretending* to rape her?"

"Believe it or not, but Lenore should know. I was lying on top of her. I don't recall being turned on by what I was doing. I think most rapists get off on the struggle, but I was too distracted by the fight to be getting any sick pleasure from her pain."

Priest nodded as if he were mulling over the information. "Pretense or not, that was a pretty deep slice in her arm, and was I mistaken, or is she getting a black eye?"

"I understand your protective nature and I respect it. She's a young woman and your friend; you want to help her; kiss her boo-boos." I could see Priest shift at the condescending undertone of his statement, but he stayed quiet. "She doesn't need a white knight. She needs to become a white knight, and unfortunately I was the dark knight hired to do the job."

"And tonight was about the job? All alone in a house with a beautiful woman who has no one to protect her. How do I know you weren't taking advantage of the situation?"

Garrett glanced to the front of the church. "Just to be clear. *You're* questioning *my* motives toward Lenore?"

Priest narrowed his eyes. "Lenore is safe here. I would never harm her."

"Safe." Garrett nodded and shuffled his feet around. "Why is everyone so eager to keep her safe? You don't protect someone from the water by never teaching them to swim. You don't protect someone from a disease by not inoculating them."

"We aren't talking about shots and floaties, Garrett!" Priest sat up and motioned to the dressing room. "You beat the crap out of her tonight and scared her half to death!"

"Yes, I did, and do you know what happened? She fought me, Matthew." Garrett brandished his sloppily bandaged hand. "She fought me, and she won. She got away. That's all I'm taking away from tonight. She might wake up tomorrow with cuts and bruises, but I don't care. Her enemies will do nothing less."

"You talk as if you are sending her into battle against an army of glimmer grim."

"Please don't make yourself the fool in this. You are a priest, after all. Do you really think this is all there is? Do you think life ends as we know it, and a few puppeteering demons show up to wreck our parties? We are headed into so much more trouble, and if you care about Lenore, you will realize she needs to get with the program. You do too, actually, but I'm not going to waste my time trying to dig you out of this hole."

"I understand your concerns for the future, and training Lenore can only help her, but why are you going to such extreme lengths to do so?"

"I've observed Lenore over the last couple weeks. She follows orders well enough, she learns quickly, but she's not a forward thinker. She's very dependent. She is, for lack of a better word, lazy." I cringed at hearing that word again. I do everything for everyone. I'm the damn kickstand. I hold everyone else up.

"Lazy? I've never observed that."

"I just mean she is willing to let others take care of her. When push comes to shove, she just falls down. She thinks nothing of losing a sword match, because it isn't going to result in her death. She doesn't worry about our mock fighting, because I'm not using my full strength. If I had tried to fight her tonight, she would have given up, or retreated, or begged me to stop."

"Lenore is not weak," Priest grumbled in my defense, though I wasn't sure he had any evidence to back it up.

Garrett cleared his throat. "I agree, but she has made assumptions about my character that prevented her from considering me dangerous. I had to threaten her with something she could believe me capable of, but something she was not willing to endure. It was a low blow, but a necessary one."

"You think if you walked up to her and slugged her, she would have cowered from you instead of fighting back?"

"I know she would have," Garrett said without a hint of doubt. I wanted it not to be true, but he was right. I already knew I wasn't a fighter, but for the first time in my life I was ashamed of that. This new world didn't leave room to distinguish between pacifists and cowards.

"What will you do next time to scare her? Try to cut off her fingers?"

"I will continue to train her harder each day. Eventually, I will be outright hitting her. She'll either fight back or have to endure the pain."

Priest crossed his arms and set his jaw. "And she's supposed to return to that voluntarily?"

"Voluntarily is a subjective term. I would like her to return by choice, but given the circumstances in the world we live in, I'm not sure voluntary will ever be the right word."

Priest stood up. The stairs offered him a good lording position to Garrett, but since Garrett was broader than him, it didn't have the desired effect.

"Lenore!" Priest called for me and I came out after a short pause. He held out his hand to me. I went to him and took it. It was all a display, but I was more than happy to participate. "Lenore can do whatever she wishes," he informed Garrett. "She may leave with you now. She may stay with me here. She may run away altogether, but one thing is certain. *You* will not be staying. Give me a few minutes with her and you'll have her answer."

Priest hugged me to him and walked me around the altar. Garrett retreated to the back of the church to give us privacy. Priest leaned against the altar, and I stood with Garrett partially in my view. "You think I should go back with him, don't you?"

"I don't care if you go with him, but you know you don't want to stay here. I'm not even sure I want to be here anymore." Priest looked around the church like he was taking in its condition for the first time. "Besides, he might be right. This glimmer grim thing may turn into something bigger. Do you want to be prepared for that?"

I shrugged. "Even if it does, it's not like I'm going to be the one to stop it. I know August thinks we can save the world or something, but I don't. It's been hell in a handbasket since this started. If the handbasket falls apart, it's just hell. Me picking up a sword isn't going to change anything."

Priest started to respond, but his eye caught something behind me. I turned around to see what he was looking at, but I didn't see anything. When I turned back, he was staring at me strangely. "What is it?" I asked.

"Nothing," he said, even though it was clearly something. "I'm hallucinating. It happens with this stuff. Look, do you want to remain with August?"

"Yes, I love her."

"I know, but is it worth getting the crap kicked out of you every day to be with her, to be part of her save-the-world team?"

"Yes," I said without pause. Priest seemed surprised and distrustful of my quick answer. "I can't explain it. She's like a mother to me. I would do anything for her. I think... I think I would die for her." The last part was as much a revelation to me as it was to Priest. He seemed unnerved by it. "Is that weird?"

"No," he answered flatly. "I had no idea you felt so strongly about her."

I looked around the church. I wondered if the pain of losing August could ever compare to Priest's pain from losing his God. "You know you don't have to stay here," I said looking back at him. "You're always welcome to stay with me; preferably without the harem or drugs."

He didn't blink at the offer. "I don't want you to die for August. I don't want you to die at all." He cupped my cheek, caressing it with his thumb. "If he can knock your gentle nature out of you, along with that damn nice streak, I'd like him to do it, but..." He dropped his hand.

"What?"

"You need to fight him. You need to fight as hard as you can."

"Yeah, I know."

"I'm serious. If you go with him right now, then you are committing to this. I can't have you coming back here complaining he hit you."

"Oh, that's nice. You're kicking me out."

Priest pressed his hand to his chest. "*I* can't watch you go through this. It breaks my heart to see you wearing bruises. Call me old-fashioned, but I think men shouldn't beat up women."

"I don't either, but... How else am I going to learn? It's not exactly a skill you can learn with an instructional video."

"No, it's not," he murmured. "Is that your decision then?"

I frowned at him. "Do you really not want to see me?"

Priest wobbled his head in neither a nod nor a head shake. "I'm still here if you need me."

I smiled and gave him a quick one-armed hug. I thanked him for the bandage. He grumbled something in response. We said our goodbyes, and I headed to the back of the church where my pseudo-rapist was waiting for me.

Dinner Take Two

T HE RIDE HOME WAS a little precarious since Garrett's motorcycle didn't offer much room for personal space. I tried to sit
without touching him, but he pulled out so sharply I was forced to
wrap an arm around his chest. I thought he had done it intentionally,
but I was certain he would have claimed otherwise.

When we got back, I came through the kitchen door and saw the
table was set neatly again, with fresh flowers in a vase. Since the house
wasn't filled with smoke, I presumed Garrett had also taken the time
to do something with the food. I hadn't even realized I had frozen
in the door until Garrett bumped me from behind. "Come on. The
mosquitoes are getting in."

I stepped in and started to head into the living room. My intention
was to go straight to bed, even though I was hungry.

"Lenore," Garrett said before I had made it to the stairs. His voice
held the same tone August's always did. It was a question, but also
a reprimand. I stopped and debated my options. Risk indigestion by
rushing through the most uncomfortable meal ever, or go hungry to
prove my point. That point being: I *could* go hungry, or I can get my
way, or I'm stubborn, or...

Forget it.

I came back into the kitchen as Garrett pulled the still warm skillet of food from the oven. I couldn't bring myself to sit down when he did. I wanted to eat somewhere else. I also wanted to ignore my cowardly instincts.

After Garrett had served both our plates, he turned in his chair to look at me. "What are you thinking right now?"

I blinked away my confusion. Why did people ask that? Did they actually want to know? No one ever really wants to know what you're thinking. "I don't want to be near you right now, but I don't want you to think I'm running away from you either."

"Are you angry at me, or afraid of me?"

I rolled my eyes. No matter which answer I chose, I was going to look like a typical emotional female. "I feel like you're more a stranger to me now than you were two weeks ago."

"That doesn't answer my question." He stood up abruptly, and I took a big step back. "That does, though." He put up a finger to pause the conversation and went outside. He returned a minute later holding hand cuffs. I took a couple vacillated steps away from him, but he shook his head. "Relax, Lenore. The handcuffs are for me. I'll give you the key, and you can take them off when you feel comfortable enough to risk it. Or until I have to pee, whichever comes first."

He tossed me the tiny key and latched the cuffs around his wrists behind his back. I scoffed at him, but he proceeded to sit down and eat from his plate like a dog. The comfort of his hands being bound, did allow me to sit down with him and eat.

After his second helping of food, Garrett leaned back in his chair and looked me over. It had bothered me that he barely acknowledged my existence over the last two weeks. Now that his stunt had made him intimately familiar with my body, I wished he *would* forget I existed.

"Do you want to hit me?" he asked when I couldn't meet his eyes.

I snorted in an attempt to laugh, but he didn't offer it as a joke, so I let my smile drop. "No, I don't want to hit you. I don't even want to be near you."

"I can't have you afraid of me."

"I thought that was the whole point. Scare me into fighting you. Scare me into survival mode."

"Yes, but it won't work twice. You won't fight me nearly as hard if you suspect I'll let up at the last second."

"I could start wearing skirts so we could skip the fight and go straight to the rape." He looked away. He was no doubt irritated, but I also detected offense. "Why is she making me do this?"

He looked back at me like I had asked him to tell me what he hides under his mattress. He thought about it a moment, before standing to retrieve his plate via his bound hands. He managed to get it off the table and slide it into the sink without breaking it.

A man cleaning up his dishes post-apocalypse? Maybe hell had frozen over. Or maybe it was just avoidance at its best.

I brought my own dish over and started a batch of soapy water in the sink. "There has to be a reason," I said to remind him he hadn't answered me yet.

"Aside from saving your life?"

"Yes," I answered. He rolled his eyes and leaned against the counter by the sink while I proceeded to wipe down the table and bring over the other dishes. "I get the purpose. I just don't get the effort." The suds in the sink mushroomed up when I dumped the skillet in. A blob of foam hit Garrett's face. He blew most of it off, but a little piece remained on his nose. I briskly wiped it off with a dry towel, which he thanked me for. He also had some remnants of sauce on his face from the meal, but not enough to be compelled to clean him.

"Why, don't you think you're worth the effort?"

"Am I?" I waved my hand to the set that had been the scene of my fake sexual assault. "Look how far you had to go to get my so-called best."

He nodded broodingly as I washed the dishes. "You did impress me tonight, though. You might be too stubborn to start a fight, but once it was out of your control, you were forceful and creative."

He turned so he wasn't relying on the counter to hold him up. His proximity put me on guard, but I held my ground. "August wants to reverse your foot-dragging obstinacy into a stalwart fighter. I thought she was wrong about you. I didn't think you were worth the effort either, but after tonight I think she may have been right. So, now that I'm on board too, you can expect to be miserable. Tomorrow I am going to make you hate me so much you'll never say no to an offer to hit me again."

"Great, I suppose I should feel privileged you are waiting that long."

He glanced over to the table. "I'd like to apologize for earlier," he said ignoring my quip. "It was a necessary performance, but that's not who I am. I expect you'll continue to hate me. That's for the best, but if you would allow it, I would like to reverse some of your impressions of me as a man."

"How's that again?" I hadn't been listening, since the skillet wasn't voluntarily releasing its dinner residue, but I probably would have asked it anyway.

"I don't mind being hated. I don't mind you being scared of me, so far as it suits your training, but I don't want to be a monster to you." He stepped away from the counter, and I turned to see what his strategy was. I must have been wearing twenty layers of dumbfounded on my face, but he seemed to be oblivious to it. "Whenever you're ready."

"Ready? What do you want me to do?"

"Come to me, so I can offer you a different picture of me. One without violence." I must have stepped back, because my butt got wet from the sink's overspill. "Please," he said lowering his head. He wasn't badgering me with an apology, because he knew I would never accept it. He was, however, offering a redo. He wanted to change how I saw him. "I'm still cuffed. I won't take advantage. I just want one kiss."

Hearing the word kiss made my whole body flare hot. It wasn't even sexual or angry heat. It was as if someone had called me in front of an audience to give a speech... in my underwear. I shook my head, but just the thought of kissing made me wet my lips. I smacked my washcloth on the counter and walked off.

I was halfway through the living room before a thought occurred to me. Maybe I needed to kiss him too. Once again, the thought wasn't based on any sexual desire I had for him. At this point, my emotions toward him were being stored in a mental file cabinet in reverse chronological order of experiences. I did feel threatened by him, though. If I ignored how I felt, it would put me on edge. That might help me train, but it would also make me worry myself into restless sleep, and gastritis-provoking mealtimes.

Garrett didn't want me to view him as a rapist bastard because he found the label offensive to his honorable nature. I didn't want to view him that way, because it would make the next few weeks or months intolerable.

After my pause in thought and step, I returned to the kitchen and found him still standing in the center of the kitchen waiting for his kiss. He didn't smile when I returned, which was good. He watched me fidget and inch toward him like he might suddenly jump me again.

When I was right in front of him, he leaned in for a kiss and I pulled away. I wasn't even sure why I did it. Somehow, in my cycle of prudishness, I forgot how to let someone kiss me. I chuckled and apologized. I looked at him to see if I had annoyed him again, but he was patiently waiting for my kiss.

My eyes watered and I shook my head. "I'm sorry," I apologized again laughing at my confusing reaction to what should have been a simple kiss. "I can do this." His brow dove deep and he tilted his head to look me over. "It's not you," I said, feeling more tears coming on. "Geez, I can't believe I'm getting this worked up. Okay, kiss me." I turned back to him, but by now he was showing concern for my sudden blubbering. "Just do it. I understand your purpose." I moved toward him to kiss him, but this time *he* pulled away.

"Would you feel comfortable uncuffing me?" I nodded and pulled out the key. Once he was free, I wiped my eyes and sniffled a few times so I wasn't the most disgusting lip partner. He put his hands on his hips and watched me prepare. "That long, huh?" he asked and I responded with a mumbled curse.

He came at me painfully slow, and put his hand around my back. He drew me forward, and I closed my eyes. I dutifully tipped up my head and parted my lips. His lips pressed against my forehead instead.

For a moment, I felt rejected, but his arms drew me in closer pressing me to his chest.

I was too tired to fight, too exhausted to delve into the strangeness of being held by a man I hated five minutes ago, and would hate again tomorrow. I relaxed against his chest and felt the warmth of his body. He smelled like the leather of his motorcycle jacket.

At what point I started sniffling out stuttered sobs I don't know, but he continued to hold me while I did. I apologized a few more times for my theatrics, but he just patted my back when I did.

When I finally pulled away from him, he pulled my matted hair away from my face and poured me a glass of water. After I guzzled it down, I waited for him to say something, but he didn't. "Do you still want your kiss?" I asked.

He smiled, or at least he almost smiled. "I think we've at least dismantled a few assumptions about my character by now. That ought to get us through the bulk of our uncomfortable silences." He moved past me, but stopped. "Unless you still want one."

I wanted to look at him. I imagined his expression might have been less pleading this time, and more hopeful. I didn't look, though. Bottom line was, he was a man, I was a woman, and we were alone together in a house full of beds. We were bound to wind up in one of them at some point. It certainly didn't have to be tonight. There was always time to explore my ever-changing opinion of his character, and my emotions that went with it.

So It Begins

T HERE'S ALWAYS A STARTING point to every story. The tale of my training with Garrett should have started two weeks ago, but it didn't. Since he had even less faith in my abilities than I did, his efforts to groom my fighting skills had thus far been perfunctory; a torpid attempt to induce my natural survival skills: kick, punch, bite, run. After the kitchen incident, he started to see my underlying skill—albeit unrefined—at thinking on my feet. That was when Garrett decided to start training me for real.

When I came downstairs and found the couch empty, I wasn't surprised. Garrett was an early riser and rarely out-slept me. He had taken to sleeping on the couch instead of a room upstairs. His excuse was that without a nightly watch rotation he needed to be our first line of defense against the grim, but I think he just wanted to keep me from sneaking off in the middle of the night.

I did however find the lack of breakfast odd. He wasn't much of a housekeeper, but either out of graciousness or expediting progress, he had been making breakfast for us. Since I didn't see him or smell Spam frying, I went to the back door to see if he was battling a trespassing grim outside.

I reached for the doorknob but it was gone. Locked or unlocked, it made no difference; the hardware within kept the door shut. Aside from the gaping hole that allowed free admission to bugs, I assumed it was an attempt at securing the house, since we were without a proper night watch. I headed to the side door in the kitchen, but that knob was gone also.

It took a lot to scare me, especially these days, but the thought of being trapped in a confined space was ranking on my "pee your pants" level. "Garrett?" I said quietly, hoping he was going to jump out and attack soon, so I could fold like a weak chair and disappoint his efforts.

I heard movement from the laundry room, just off the back of the living room. The room had nothing to be frightened of, except it led to the basement, the place where our deceased resident was stored.

The former elderly man should have been subdued by my holy water, but the process did require fairly regular updates to prevent emergence. It was the downside of keeping bodies in the home, but it was an unwritten rule if we took a house, we had to protect the residents from changing. It *seemed* noble—past tense included.

I decided, with the little bravery I had, to go check it out. I was confident the resident was secure. I assumed it was Garrett, planning a sneak attack.

As I rounded the corner to the little room, I discovered I was right and wrong. The resident of the house was still securely padlocked in the basement. The crystallized man before me was a completely different grim.

The one thing difficult to agree on when it came to grim was how to deal with them. Many people argued the bodies of the risen should be preserved. These type of people usually stayed hidden in their homes

23 hours a day, living on whatever creature happened to wander into their traps. They were also the type of people that, despite their conviction to protect the grim, would freely shoot *living* trespassers like they were part of a carnival game.

Damn hicks.

August and the others took to killing the grim for sport. The only rule: the grim had to be animated. They considered it unethical to dismantle a body that hadn't tried to hurt anyone yet. It was a strange morality, especially since all the crystalline dead had the potential to become grim. But, once again, in a world without social taboos, we started to develop our own criteria for behavior. We unwittingly wanted to be restricted. It was the only thing keeping us out of the dangerous *Lord of the Flies* territory.

Which brings me back to the growling, glaring, human-wearing demon standing between me and my washing machine. My sympathies for the consecrated body he inhabited went right out the window the moment he exposed his teeth. The fine-pointed, jagged dentition in his mouth was handcrafted. It told me this demon was especially maniacal. It also told me he had full control over the faculties of this body.

Screaming would have been an appropriate response, but in situations where legs are far more vital than voice boxes, you tend to forget that part.

I ran from the room barely escaping whatever was thrown after me. I rounded the corner with only three thoughts: knife, screwdriver, bedroom.

To break that down for you, I gave myself three options to survive. The first of course was to fight—*yeah right*. The second was to find a screwdriver and twist the remaining hardware in the door in order to escape—not enough time. The third option was to run up to my bedroom and hide behind a locked door.

In truth, I wanted to go hide. Two weeks ago, and maybe even one day ago, I might still have done that, but I already knew the only weapons I had up there were toxic hairsprays and girdles. If they hadn't killed women this far in, they weren't likely to take down a grim.

My hair snagged on something as I changed directions at the last second to head to the kitchen. The pain was easily ignored. I didn't bother turning to see how close he was. I was already moving at the impossible speed of Mach-*holy shit.*

I reached the knife block and found the only knife left in it. Garrett had most likely removed the others so the grim didn't follow my lead. I flung the block behind me, unsheathing my weapon in the process. As I rounded the island, I grabbed the skillet drying by the sink.

There was no guarantee of anything at that point, but I knew my speed wouldn't hold out. Getting trapped in a smaller room upstairs wasn't going to help me either. I needed to turn around and face the grim truth. Pun intended.

I swung the skillet as I turned. The pan chipped the grim's face. With my retreat at an end, he reached for me, but I dodged his grasp and stabbed his hand. Though the grim didn't feel pain, he did take the slightest inventory of his now missing finger.

While he was preoccupied, I kicked out his knee. He stumbled back on his damaged leg. I flung the skillet at his head. His skull fractured, but it wasn't enough to displace the demon. I toppled onto him, pinned him to the floor, and proceeded to stab him every which way

I could manage. At some point his neck crumbled away and his growl quieted.

I panted over my bloodless kill with a strange satisfaction. A slow clap brought my attention back to the room. Garrett had returned and was standing over me like a proud teacher. His mouth wasn't smiling, but his eyes were.

I dove at him, sans knife. He must have expected the attack, because he caught my arms and hastened my descent to the floor on the other side of him. He didn't retaliate, but he did ready himself for another round. "You're not ready to fight me," he said flatly when I gripped the skillet on the floor beside me.

"I hate you," I snarled.

He relaxed his stance and offered me a hand up. "That's okay."

I took the proffered hand out of some sense of truce, and he pulled me up. I started to walk away, but he didn't let go of my arm. I expected to see a coy smile on his face, something indicating that he wasn't ready to let go of my hand.

A few too many romance novel scenes later, and I was twisted up in his arms with one of the missing kitchen knives at my throat. "You didn't think it would be that easy, did you?" he murmured in my ear. Apparently, breakfast wasn't just postponed, but canceled.

The Middle

A MONTH LATER, MY skills should have been improving, but they weren't. Garrett insisted they were, but he was still beating me hand over fist... literally. I was covered in bruises and slashes. I was the poster child for abused women: beaten to a bloody pulp and still going back for more.

I wanted to win more than ever, for myself, but I still couldn't beat him. My sword fighting was laughable, and even Garrett admitted we were probably wasting our time trying to force skill where there wasn't talent. My running speed had improved, as well as my jumping, but no matter how fast I was, I still couldn't beat him in hand-to-hand combat.

I flew back feeling the full impact of his fist on my eye. It was astonishing how much it hurt to be punched in the face. I was certain my eye might explode like a water balloon, but it never did. The swelling would go down. The black eyes would fade, although they were usually quickly replaced.

Normally—in regards to my *new* normal—I would have gotten right back up and gone after him, but this time I just stayed down. We had been sparring for an hour, working our way up to real hits as a way to build endurance to pain. Basically, we were beating the crap out of each other. Obviously I was losing.

"Get up," Garrett bellowed in his deepest commanding voice. I could tell he was angry. He was getting more temperamental every day. I assumed he was as frustrated with my progress as I was, but his displeasure wasn't going to make me fight harder. Hell, he was already hitting me daily; what more could he threaten me with? "Get up!" he yelled.

I opened one eye, since the other was already swelling shut. He was panting. At least he had to exert some effort to defeat me. I shook my head with lazy defiance. He clenched his teeth and huffed his derision like a big-nosed bull.

When his leer didn't move me, he kicked my leg. It hurt, but not enough for me to give him the satisfaction of winning. When I mouthed, "fuck you" at him, I could almost see the steam coming out of his ears.

He knelt down beside me and grabbed me by my shirt. I wasn't surprised he had the strength to pull my torso off the ground, but I was impressed my cotton shirt didn't rip in his grip. "That's a great idea. Maybe since you're just going to lie on your back, I can get a little use out of you."

He tried to look me over luridly, but his eyes too quickly came back to rest on mine. It was only a threat. He might have wanted to do just that, but from what I had gleaned from his closed-mouth personality over the last six weeks, he was bashful when it came to sex.

More than a few nights I had fallen asleep on the couch with him, and each time he delivered me to my bedroom without any attempt to do more. I had even gotten brave enough to walk around the house in my towel after my shower, but he didn't take the bait. For the most part, I still hated him, but I was starved for attention. Even the potential of having sex was better than nothing at all.

I smiled up at Garrett's leering face. "As long as I don't have to move, you can do whatever you want."

His face contorted between three or four confused and menacing expressions before he settled on interest. His eyes flickered over mine, trying to read me. Was I being a smart-ass, or did I genuinely not mind if he had me? He couldn't read me, so he looked over my body.

He was evaluating me. Seeing how much he wanted me. Was it worth throwing out the whole day's schedule just to satisfy his needs? Adding to that, was it worth potentially disrupting days and weeks after if he wanted more?

I hated to interrupt the questions lining up on his face. I probably needed and wanted sex even more than he did, but I also needed and wanted to win one freaking battle. I wasn't an egotist, but I was a feminist, so for the remainder of female-kind, I wanted to beat him.

The rock I had been slowly wiggling loose beside me, just out of his line of sight, was a decent handful. Once I got my grip on it, I flung my hand up and thwacked his skull. I was careful not to hit his temple, but I held nothing back on my strength.

Before he could recover from the blow, I punched him with my other fist, and kicked him back. I jumped on top of him, gut-punching him with my weight. I hit him with the rock again, which made his eyes roll back, followed shortly after by his head. Once I was sure he was knocked out and not pretending, I did a long victory lap around the yard, *Rocky*-style.

After that I checked to see if he was still breathing.

The Humbled and the Proud

"WHAT UP MY BITCH?" I chimed as Garrett walked into the kitchen with my homemade bandage around his head. He had been out for several hours, and I was really starting to worry, but instead of fretting, I cranked up Jimmy the Card's evening request hour. I had called in several requests in honor of my low-blow win, but so far Jimmy wasn't playing anything he didn't want to, which was often the case with him. His radio, his rules.

Garrett perked an eyebrow at my rap-stimulated dialogue. I laughed at him, and continued to make a batch of tuna helper. "How's your eye?" he murmured.

I couldn't help but chuckle at the endearing question. I had black eyes from the moment we started this endeavor, and he never asked about them. "Swelling nicely. If you're planning another attack, I would advise coming from my right, since I have virtually no peripheral vision. What about you? Are you going to live?"

I looked him over. Concussions were dangerous, since doctors were few and far between. The fact that he was talking and walking was a good thing.

"Headache, but no more than I've had before. I should live."

"So, I don't have to feel guilty about bragging my success over the airwaves," I said, adding a little shoulder dance to my vaunting.

"I'd be disappointed if you didn't," he said. "You did well. Perhaps not the traditional gentleman's method of fighting, but clearly grim aren't gentlemen." I shook my head in agreement, before adding my tuna to the skillet. "Can I help you with anything?" he asked.

I raised my brow at him. "I don't think I've ever heard those words spoken in this kitchen."

Garrett nodded and came up behind me. For a moment, once again betrayed by the visions of romantic novels forever stained on my brain, I thought he might have intended to rub my shoulders, or kiss my neck. Instead, he took my wooden spoon and gently shoved me aside.

Not sure what to do, I leaned on the island and watched him do my job. He immediately adjusted the heat on the pan and added more water. At first I thought he was doing it to look like he knew what he was doing, but it was clear after he started doctoring with spices that he was familiar with cooking.

"If I had known all I had to do to get help in the kitchen was beat someone up, I would have done it sooner." He smirked at me, which pleased me even more than my earlier victory. He tasted the sauce and nodded in approval. "Am I that bad of a cook?" I asked as an afterthought. He dipped the spoon back in and gave me a come-hither finger with his free hand. I moved to slurp the hot liquid and nodded. "I am that bad of a cook."

"Not bad. You haven't killed anyone, have you?" His smirk had long since disappeared, but I could see a slight sparkle in his eyes that told me he was seeing me much differently post goose egg. Apparently I was trying to get his attention in all the wrong ways.

"With my food, no. I doubt August would have let me join if I had." I moved to the table and sat down with my feet propped up. It was only dinner, but it felt like pampering.

"You do realize she didn't bring you in just to cook and clean," Garrett said, turning more attention to me than the skillet.

"Of course she did. I'm the non-fighter. What else am I going to do to earn my keep?"

"First off, *no*, she didn't. She invited you into the group because you were clearly lonely and needed some friends." I crossed my arms like being accused of loneliness was something to be ashamed of. "Second, you are officially a fighter." He pointed to his own black eye. "Third, and most important, you don't have to earn my sister's friendship to keep it. She loves unconditionally."

"Then why didn't she say something? I've been cooking and cleaning for them since I joined."

"Well," Garrett smirked, "she's not stupid." I let my mouth hang open as I thought about how many times I wished someone would clean up after themselves. Apparently they might have, if I hadn't been doing it for them. "You should have been a little worse at cooking; then she would have offered more help."

I scoffed and threw a bundle of napkins off the table at him. He smiled at the pubescent attack. It was a real smile, one I hadn't seen before. It made his hard muscular face seem softer. He looked younger when he smiled. To my dismay it didn't last, though; he was back to stirring the supper before I could prolong the flirtation.

Are we done yet?

I T HAD BEEN NEARLY three months since I had been left with Garrett to train. Our living arrangement was starting to grate on me. He was starting to open up, and be friendlier, but he was still a boring companion. He wouldn't reveal too much about himself, and in the end, what little attraction I had for him was turned off by his distance.

When the rain came, I thought cabin fever might force him to converse more, but he had other plans. "Here, put this on." Garrett threw a poncho at me.

My jaw ceased mid-chew, and I stared at the plastic coat. "What for?"

"You'll want to stay dry if possible. Training in the rain sucks."

"It's not raining, it's pouring."

"Yeah, but you aren't going to be snoring," he quipped dead-pan.

I proceeded to nibble on my not-so-lucky charms like he wasn't there. His patience was always paper-thin, but he waited for me to finish my meal before pulling my bowl from me. I took as much time as I needed and wanted to get my shoes and poncho on. All the while, Garrett was threatening a tantrum.

When I finally met him at the door, he looked like he was struggling not to blow up over such a trifling thing as my slow-motion morning starts. I twisted my mouth, sucking the last bits of yellow stars and green clovers from my teeth. "Well let's get out there, pokey." I motioned to the door without any hint of humor in my voice. Instead of glaring at my sardonic humor like I expected him to, he smiled. My face scrunched in confusion at the anomaly. "What's so funny?"

"Just for that, I'm going to work you until you puke."

"Ah, the bulimia workout today. Fun."

"Are you ever going to take this seriously?" he asked.

"Are you ever going to not take it seriously?" I asked. He shook his head. "Well, then somebody's got to put some personality into the mix." He looked me over like he wanted to respond, but he just opened the door for me to exit.

The rain was coming down hard and fast. My poncho kept my shirt dry, but since the yard was saturated, there was no hope of keeping my shoes and pants dry. "This won't last long. We can wait until it's done." I turned to see Garrett's refusal for myself, but he wasn't behind me. "Damn it." I whipped around, offering the sheeting veil around me a cursory glance, but he wasn't anywhere in sight.

I already knew this wasn't going to be fun. Somewhere between looking for a weapon and wondering if my shoes were machine washable, I was pushed to the ground. I flipped over to defend myself, but he was gone.

I got to my feet and scanned again. Aside from the yard directly around the house, we didn't mow down much of the acreage. The foliage on the outskirts had taken over in short order. An abundance of lilac bushes and cedar trees had staked a claim on anything we left alone. At that point, I could barely see beyond the rain anyway.

I was pushed down again before I even finished my scan. I jumped up, hoping to catch his escape, but he was gone. I ran from my sitting duck spot in search of solace. I hid myself behind a bundle of fountain grass.

I waited there for some time, before my feet were kicked out beneath me. I face-planted in the mud. This time I didn't bother getting up fast. Garrett had established his game. He was going to bowl me over like an overeager dog until I stopped him. Every time he managed to knock me down, I should consider myself dead.

Since remaining dry was no longer a task I could accomplish, I ripped off the poncho. With it off, I had far better hearing and vision. I wondered if Garrett had intended for me to figure that out.

Rather than staying in one spot, I moved swiftly from bush to bush, and in and out of the tall grasses. I wasn't sure if it served any purpose, but it would look good until I figured out something tactical to do.

My butt burned from a drive-by spanking. I caught a glimpse of Garrett running away and I bolted after him. If he was the runaway dog, then I could be a dog-catcher. He glanced back and saw me coming up to him. He made a quick turn through a white trellis arch to evade me.

I followed the bush line and ran through the arch after him. His arm shot out of nowhere and clotheslined me. My back slammed into the wet ground with a splosh. I could barely breathe and by the time I could, he was gone again.

I cursed and got up. I padded back to the middle of the yard and waited. Hiding wasn't doing me any good. I might as well go back to what worked for me: being bait.

I braced myself for an attack and waited. I couldn't rely on my sight, since I was practically standing under a waterfall. I could barely hear over the downpour. I couldn't outrun him. I had only one option left: my brain.

I was doomed.

I stood facing the driveway. The house was to my left and the bulk of the foliage to my back. The yard stretched out significantly farther to my right, which meant he would be exposed longer from that direction. He would almost certainly approach me from behind. And after his attack, he would likely angle toward the house, for a quick escape.

That sounded smart, right?

I heard the sloshing of footsteps when he was practically on top of me. I didn't hesitate. I dropped low, throwing out my left leg to the side. He missed his target, tripped over my extended leg, and skidded through the wet grass.

Not entirely satisfied with my win, I leapt on top of him and straddled his chest. I pinned his arms with my knees using my weight to hold him down. He tried to bring his legs up to lasso my neck, but I hit him with a hard crotch shot. He coughed and spluttered. He didn't want to show his pain, but he didn't have much of a choice.

I could see his eyes searching for an escape. I held up my fist to his face. "Move and I make you a falsetto." He relaxed his head back and let his arms give up the struggle. "Do I win?"

"You already lost four times. We can go again and if you beat me another three times, then we can call it a draw."

Without warning I punched him in the crotch again. He groaned and huffed in shock at my unnecessary violence. I was surprised by it myself, but I was sick of the training. I was sick of him looking down at me. I was also sick of having the crap beat out of me without retribution. "What the hell, Lenore?" he croaked.

"Do I win?" I yelled in his face. He looked confused, so I punched him in the jaw. His confusion was replaced by a fresh batch of shocked anger. "Are we done?" I hit him again, even though his face felt like a brick wall.

I wasn't sure what he saw in my expression to wipe away the fury on his face, but it died back as swiftly as it came. When he didn't concede, I moved to punch him in the face again. I had no purpose. I just wanted to hurt him.

"Okay!" he interrupted my violent enthusiasm to save himself the pain. "You win, Lenore!" My hand was still primed, but it was shaking. I didn't want to put it down. I knew he was only trying to appease me, to keep me from beating in his face any further. I hadn't won.

Nothing about the last three months was a win.

"I hate you," I hissed. "Everything is different because of you. I liked the way things were. I was happy. I was *happy*, you bastard!"

"Lenore." I could hear the paternal tone in his voice. He was trying to talk a jumper off a ledge. I moved off of him before I could hear his pathetic negotiations for my calmness.

It wouldn't have helped anyway. I was finally mad. I was hurt when August left me. I was afraid when Garrett pretended to rape me. I was frustrated the first time he gave me a black eye, and the subsequent dozen. I had spent more than enough time being sad and scared. It was time to be angry, and I didn't want him to talk me out it.

I stalked off with no particular direction in mind. I wanted to go see Priest, but he didn't need or want to see my latest battle wounds. I walked along the road in the faint hope that I could just keep walking. I still wasn't brave enough for that, but it was a coward's dream. I managed to make it half a mile before Garrett's motorcycle rumbled up behind me.

He slowed to a stop ahead of me and pulled off his helmet. The rain had let up and I could see he was starting to get a faint black eye where my second punch had hit him, but it wasn't nearly as big as I would have preferred. "You'll catch a cold out here," he said, attempting to be playful.

I stopped and stared him down. I wanted to say something, but I ended up waiting him out. I had talked enough for the both of us. He could try to get a conversation rolling for once.

"Why don't you let me take you back, Lenore? A shower and some warm soup, how does that sound?"

"Like placation. Like appeasement. Like a bribe. I'm done, Garrett. Everyone has their bad days, but I'm tired of this. I'm tired of you. I want my life back. The apocalypse sucks enough. I'm not going to spend every waking moment preparing for the worst case scenario."

"If you want to survive—"

"Survive? No one gives a shit about that! The world is full of people who didn't survive, and I envy them! I would have preferred to be on the first bus out of here, but if there is another one coming, then bring it on, because I don't much care anymore!"

Garrett looked at his feet, hiding his exasperation. "Are you giving up?"

"I gave up the day I figured out *my* God left me here." My eyes watered with the thought of abandonment from a being I'd never met. It shouldn't have mattered, but it did. Admitting to Garrett I wasn't an atheist probably wasn't wise, but I didn't care anymore. "You can belittle me all you want about it, but I'm not a coward, and I'm *not* lazy. I just don't care." I started to walk away.

"That's why she chose you."

I stopped. "Because I don't care?" I sneered.

"No, because you do care. You care that He left you." I didn't respond. He got off his bike and met me in the road. "You don't have to fight for Him, though. You can fight for August. You can fight for me. It doesn't matter, because in the end, you're just fighting for yourself." He put his hand out and I stared at it.

"I'm not going back. I'm sick of fighting you."

"Good, because my jaw hurts like hell. Remind me not to piss you off again." He winked at me and I couldn't help but smile because it reminded me of Devin, which conversely made me sad again. "Come on. Let me buy you something pretty to make up for the last three months."

I rolled my eyes, but eventually he lured me onto his bike. He took off fast, and I was forced to hang on tight. I gave into it, though, because he was warm and the wind on my wet clothes was making me cold. Instead of heading home, we went into town.

Shopping Around

BY THE TIME I came out of the dressing room, Garrett had found a chair he could lounge in. My selection of blue jeans and sweatshirt made him wrinkle his nose. "I thought the intention was to buy you something pretty?"

"You can buy me something pretty, but I still need dry clothes to wear home so my ass doesn't freeze to your motorcycle seat."

"Fair enough, why don't you try on a dress next?"

I wrinkled my nose this time. "I don't like dresses."

"And yet when I first met you, you were wearing one."

"That's different. I was... drunk."

"Oh, I see. If I remember correctly, it didn't fit you that well."

"It fit too well," I mumbled, ripping the tag from my sweatshirt.

"Pick out a new one. One you can breathe in." I perked an eyebrow at him. He shrugged. "Humor me. I need a little entertainment. A fashion show hardly compares to football, but beggars can't be choosers."

I looked around the room and found a display of dresses. I nodded to them. "You can't choose football, but I'll let you choose the dress."

He smirked. "The blue one," he said without even looking over to the rack.

I tracked down a blue dress in my size and tried it on. It wasn't my style, in that it wasn't machine washable, but it did look good on me. It was a nice length and the low back gave me the opportunity to go bra-less. Every woman's dream.

I came out and twirled for Garrett. "That'll do."

I resisted the urge to say anything, but I couldn't help but scoff at his failed attempt at flattery. He either wasn't as keen on the blue dress as he thought he would be, or he just didn't want to let me know it.

"Now try on the pink one," he said again without looking at the rack.

I glanced over at the dresses. "There are no pink ones."

"On that rack." He motioned to my other side.

I shook my head. "That's not a dress, that's a negligee."

"I don't speak French. Will it fit?"

"Why would I get a satin nightgown? They're hot in the summer and freezing in winter." I crossed my arms. I was almost positive this was him flirting, but he might have just wanted to amuse himself with a live Victoria Secret commercial.

"Don't you want something to wear when Devin gets back? I assume you want to finish what you started with him that night by the fire."

I shrugged and went back into the dressing room to change. For some men there was a fine line between flirting and teasing; this was leaning toward teasing and I wasn't going to play along. I had plenty of things to make fun of myself for, and I didn't need his help.

"Or did I read that wrong?" he asked from outside. "I'm not the best at interpreting women, but I kind of got the impression you liked him."

"We aren't a couple or anything. Devin isn't that type of guy."

"Yeah, I know he studs out, but that doesn't answer my question. Is he your stud?"

I debated on telling him it was none of his business, but since he was making it his business, perhaps he had a reason to know. "No, he's not."

The pink nightgown dropped over the top of the door onto my head. "You want him to be though, don't you?"

"I don't know. It's complicated." I slipped into the nightgown even though I knew I would never wear it. "Why do you care? Since when do you follow soap operas?"

"Are you trying that on or not?"

"Yes, hang on." I adjusted the fabric so it didn't cling too tightly to anything that didn't need emphasis and opened the door. "There, happy?" I stayed inside the dressing room so I could retreat as soon as he was finished ogling me.

He was back in his chair, leaning his face into his hand like he was bored to death. After a moment of gawking, he took in a deep breath and shook his head. "No, you're right. You don't want that."

I slammed the door and changed back into my jeans and sweatshirt. When I came out with my wet clothes in hand and no blue dress, Garrett went back in to grab it. I glared at him. "I'll never wear that," I griped.

"Yes, you will," he said, hooking me around the back and ushering me to the front counter.

"No, I won't."

Garrett slipped behind the counter and folded the dress neatly into tissue paper. "One night when Devin is back, you'll get the nerve up to knock on his door. He won't be able to resist you in this." He tucked the wrapped dress into a bag.

"Says the man with the high compliment of 'that'll do.'"

He handed me the bag and moved back around to my side. "It will do... for Devin." He leaned against the counter next to me and stared me down.

I furrowed my brow. "I'm missing something. You don't like the blue dress personally, but you think Devin will."

"Well, that's what this is about, isn't it? Attracting Devin?"

I looked down at the bag in my hand like it was a trap waiting to be unleashed. I shook my head. "I thought this was about you sucking up so I don't punch you in the jaw again."

"Sure, coming to get the dress was about that. Getting you out of the house to depressurize your steam was about that. The choice of dress is about attracting attention. Whose attention depends on what you buy."

I started to speak, but I couldn't figure out how to ask what I wanted to ask without making it entirely obvious what I was asking. Garrett patiently watched me, waiting for my gaping mouth to serve some purpose. He, on the other hand, wasn't flustered in the least by the topic of conversation.

"Who...?" I tried, but stopped. "Why do you think Devin will like the blue one?"

"Because he likes a dolled-up woman. He likes dresses, perfume, makeup, and all that bullshit."

"Do you think Devin would like the pink one?" Garrett shook his head slowly with a hint of severity in his eyes. "Would anyone like the pink one?" He nodded his head slowly, refusing to grant me any help in translating his message. "You didn't like the pink one." I frowned.

"I didn't say that. I said *you* don't want the pink one. Unless I read you wrong. As I said, I'm not good at reading women." He grabbed the bag from me. "I'll put this in my satchel. Bag up those wet clothes before you bring them out."

I stood by the counter after he left, trying to figure out how blue and pink had become such a difficult decision.

Cupid's Arrows

DESPITE GARRETT'S OBVIOUS HINT about choosing him over Devin, he hadn't made any attempts to seduce me beyond being a little less brusque. I had all but refused to do any more training, but he talked me into working on my archery skills. Since I was already good at that, I didn't feel like it would be too much trouble.

Famous last words.

"Five. Eight. Twelve. Six. Two. Two! Faster Lenore!"

"I'm dizzy!" I said after the second attempt at the two o'clock target went into the cab of a rusted-out car instead of in the circle drawn on the door. I put the bow down and closed my eyes.

"Lenore." My name was more often a scold than an address from him.

"I can't go that fast."

"Turn your head first and then your body," he said, manually turning my neck and then forcefully turning my hips. It made me falter, but he held me up.

"Okay!" I screamed at him and took a few deep inhalations that didn't help the dizziness, but kept me from punching him again.

"Are you ready?" he asked, walking out in front of me.

"I think so."

"Are you ready?"

"Yes!" I yelled. "Are you going to move, so I don't hit you?"

"If you're as good as you claim, then you shouldn't hit me."

"Are you willing to bet your life on that?"

"Yes," he said without hesitation. I frowned at him for the overconfidence. "Nine!"

He continued to yell out the numbers and I proceeded to pull arrows and fire. I slowed when I had to hit a target near him, but the extra half second ensured a bullseye. I managed to increase the speed between the targets while still getting a good aim. When all the arrows were used we collected them again.

"You are pretty good," Garrett said as we came back to my mark.

"Ooh, a compliment; are you sure my ego won't burst my head? I'm surprised you haven't erupted into flames for offering it."

"That's funny, Lenore," he said, stone-faced.

"Is it? I can't tell, Tin Man."

He shoved the arrows into my quiver. "Just because I don't guffaw like a jackass, doesn't mean I don't have a sense of humor. Line up to the twelve o'clock target."

"Guffaw!" I snorted and adjusted my position. "Shit, I'd be happy with a smile."

"I said line up." Garrett jerked my hips to a closed stance despite my preference for an open stance. "What is this, day one of archery class?"

"Yes, sir." I saluted. "Would you like me to lick your boots, sir?"

Garrett repositioned and presented me with a fake smile. "How's that?"

"That'll do," I mocked, turning his phrase back on him.

"Damn, you're spicy today. Anything in particular bothering you, other than my demeanor?" He raised his hand to his ear when I didn't say anything. "So, nothing else is bothering you other than me being me?" I shook my head. "How about this, Lenore? How about you straighten your damn shoulders and shoot the target." He pointed to the target like I might have been confused as to what a target was. "Every last arrow, as straight and true as you are capable."

"That's it? Loose my arrows at one target. What's the catch?"

"The catch is I'm going to be distracting you. Don't pay attention to me, just shoot. If you go outside the target line even once, then you cook and clean tonight. Deal?"

"Deal," I said, confident in my skills. "Tell me when to start."

Garrett moved around behind me and gave me the go-ahead. I managed to get two clean shots off as he clapped his hands by my ears. He pulled a cluster of hair from my head, but I hit my target.

For an arrow or two, he did nothing and I braced myself for something painful. When I felt him press his body against mine, I floundered for a moment. "Keep shooting. Pause and you forfeit," Garrett warned.

I shot true even when his hands reached under my shirt to caress my stomach. He pinched me hard, but I ignored it. I could see his plan and I wasn't going to let him distract me with pleasure or pain.

I cleared my mind of assumptions and pressed on to finish my task. When he kissed the back of my neck, I nearly fell over from shock, but the arrow made it to the target. Barely.

His hand went farther up my shirt, not bothering to stop at threatening the gates of the castle. "What...?" Was all I got out.

"Keep shooting," he whispered as he caressed my breasts, teasing my nipples.

I couldn't believe how far he was taking his challenge. I also couldn't believe I was letting him. Cooking and cleaning didn't suck enough to be manhandled in this way—not that I wasn't enjoying it. My arrow hit the bullseye, which surprised even me.

"That's good, Lenore; three more arrows. Do you want to quit?"

I grabbed for another arrow and his hands went back down my shirt. I hit the target. He skirted the waistband of my jeans, but he kept his hands above the denim as he traveled down. I hit the target, but just. I reached for the last arrow and I could feel my hands shaking. I was fully aware that I was taking a little longer nocking the last arrow.

I took my aim as his hands gripped my thighs just outside of where I wanted them. I held my breath for the release and out of anticipation. He backed away right before I shot the arrow. The sudden lack of support behind me made me aware of how much I was leaning against him. I faltered and my aim suffered for it. The arrow landed in the grass behind the target.

"Oh, too bad." Garrett smiled at me. "You were this close." He displayed his nearly closed fingers for effect. "How unsatisfying for you."

I'm not sure what glaring expression I wanted to offer, but the smile on his face which was at my expense was snuffing out my anger with another emotion. I nodded. "Yeah." I headed to the house, not bothering to collect my arrows.

"We aren't done," Garrett called after me.

"Yes." I turned to face him so he could see how serious I was. "We are. I'll fix dinner and I'll clean up, but I want you out of my house tomorrow morning. I can tolerate the bruises. I can live with your cold, uncommunicative personality. But I won't stand for this teasing game. I'm not lonely enough for that."

He didn't offer the sheepish look I expected. He looked stoic as usual.

The Last Supper

I MADE A QUICK meal of Spaghetti O's and Vienna sausages. It was hardly a meal fit for an adult, but I didn't want too many dishes and I didn't want to spend more than a few minutes preparing it.

I was surprised Garrett had no objections about leaving. He packed up his bag and set it by the door like he planned to leave that night instead of in the morning. When he came back in with his jacket on, I expected he might skip the meal as well.

He looked over the microwaved meal with disdain before looking to me. I didn't offer anything that might be construed as an opening for appeal. He came in and sat down at the table. He didn't bother offering the standard "looks good" before diving in with his spoon.

It was apparently a race against awkwardness, so he didn't bother to swallow between bites. The faster he ate the more my stomach felt too sick to eat. I knew we had gotten off to a rocky start. I also knew he wasn't a great conversationalist, but I thought perhaps he might attempt to mend the situation. I watched him practically choke himself to get through our last meal together and it made me feel like a piece of gum on the bottom of his shoe.

I didn't bother excusing myself when my eyes started to water. I slipped away from the table and went upstairs to my bedroom. As much as I wanted him to be gone, I still hated hearing the front door slam shut.

I buried my head in my pillow so I didn't have to hear his motorcycle distancing the house. I tried to remind myself I wasn't alone. My friends would be back, hopefully soon. Garrett was a difficult man to get to know, but he was still a better conversationalist than the walls.

"You forgot to take your bags out of the satchel," Garrett's muffled voice said from inside my room. I lifted my head from beneath my pillow. I was certain he could see my tears, because he already looked uncomfortable. My hair was no doubt a mess from the pillow, but that was nothing to fuss about now. "Your clothes," he said, waving two bags from the clothing store we had gone to the other day.

"Just put them anywhere," I said, baffled that he was making the effort to bring them upstairs when he could have left them downstairs, or strewn them through the yard if he preferred.

He dropped the bags right below him, taking the "anywhere" part literally. "What about this one?" He pulled a similar, but smaller bag out from under his jacket. I recognized it immediately. It had been stashed in with my wet clothes. "What do you want to do about this bag?"

"I don't know."

He pulled the pink nightgown out of the bag and dangled it on one finger. "What are we going to do about this?"

"I don't know," I said again, irritated that I was on trial for having the pink nightie when he was the one who had put every last innuendo into the damn thing.

"This is a beautiful nightgown, but I can't keep it."

"I'm not asking you to." My brow wrinkled with confusion.

"I like the way it feels," he continued with his speech. "I like the way it moves. I would love to lie next to this nightgown night after night, but I don't have that to offer."

I took in a deep breath as I gleaned the meaning of his words. "You're only here to train me. You're going back to Chicago when we're done, aren't you?" He nodded. "When?"

"Not long. I've been wanting to explore this, but for reasons even beyond time limits, I didn't think that was fair to you. I see my waffling has made me seem like a tease. I'm sorry for that. I didn't mean to put you on the rollercoaster with me." He stepped forward and handed me the negligee and sat on the bed with me. "I didn't argue with you about leaving because I thought it might be best to leave before I make you hate me for more reasons than you already do. The truth is, you either need to put that on, or I need to get the hell out of here. Either way, I'm still going to be the son of a bitch who runs out on you."

I looked down at the nightgown. I already knew what the answer was. I still had mixed feelings about Garrett's personality and his motives, but in the end there weren't a lot of men to choose from in the new world. One-night stands and flings were about as good as it got.

"Will you ever leave Chicago?"

Garrett took my hand. "I have responsibilities there." I glanced down at his hand.

"So, I shouldn't turn down all the marriage proposals I get after you leave." He smiled and even chuckled at that, but didn't answer.

I stood up and took the nightgown behind the door of my closet to slip it on. When I emerged, I saw Garrett lighting the emergency candle I kept beside my bed. It was a small gesture of romance, and I appreciated it.

He looked me over with tensed urgent attraction. It had been a long time since any man had looked at me that way, if ever. When he pulled me to straddle his lap, my hands started to shake.

"Are you okay?"

"Yes," I said with a tremor in my voice. "I didn't get a lot of practice with sex prior to the world ending."

"Oh," he said, leaning back on the bed. "It's a good thing I'm your trainer then."

I smiled and leaned over to kiss him. He tasted like mint, and I wondered if he had popped a Tic Tac on the off chance I might put on the nightgown. When he finally pulled me back from the kiss, he proceeded to instruct me on what to do, starting with removing his pants.

At first, I thought the act seemed a little too directed and unromantic, but since my past experiences were hardly worth mentioning, anything was an improvement.

We experimented with several different positions until I found one that did for me what any position did for him. He brought me the satisfaction I had been missing from my other experiences.

"Thank you," I panted into his ear, still dizzy from euphoria.

He chuckled and caressed my cheek. "You say that like we're done. Always trying to get out of your training early." He clicked his tongue.

"I hope this isn't a *work-me-until-I-puke* training session."

"No, but I'm pretty sure I can get you to the pass-out stage." He kissed me deeply. It took a moment before I could get used to the fervor of it, but once I did I was offering it right back.

One-Night Stand

THERE ARE DETAILS IN conversations you often miss the first time. It isn't until you go back over the dialogue that you notice what you missed. Garrett had been completely honest with me about not being able to stay with me. He said he would have to go back to Chicago. He also said we didn't have long. Little did I know that meant he was going to leave immediately after I fell asleep from our lovemaking.

It was alarming at first. I kept looking for him, in case he was hiding somewhere in the house. When the day went by without his return, it was clear he wasn't out getting supplies. When he wasn't back the next day it was also clear I might run out of supplies and I had no transportation to get more.

I built up a warm fire on that second night and planned out my journey to see Priest the next day. To my knowledge, he didn't have a vehicle, but I assumed one of his harem could give me a lift into town. If their drugged stupor didn't land us in a ditch, I might survive another week on my own.

When I heard the Dodge truck pull into the drive my heart leapt. I peeked out the kitchen window and saw the four-wheeler loaded in the back. There was no sign of the motorbike. That meant Devin and

Haden were back, but not August. I watched them both climb out of the cab, arguing about something. I resisted the urge to run out and greet them. It had been a hard three months for me, and an even harder last week, so I wasn't going to make them feel like heroes just for coming home.

I moved back to the fire and warmed my hands. Devin stormed in like he had never left. "I don't care, I won fair and square. Lenore!" He caught sight of me and rushed over. I couldn't keep from smiling at his energy. He picked me up in an all-encompassing hug and twirled me. "Oh, sweet thing, I missed you." He set me down and kissed me. It was a wetter kiss than I expected, but I didn't pull away. "Did you miss me?" he asked, still holding my face.

"Endlessly."

He smiled and pulled me into an even tighter hug. "Are you okay?" he whispered in my ear.

"Yeah," I whispered back.

He pulled away again. "You would not believe how much fun I had. We went to the tournaments in the Metro, I competed and I won!" He did a little dance to show his enthusiasm.

"Devin," August's voice carried over from the kitchen door. "We can talk about all that later."

My heroine looked serene and magnanimous as usual, but seeing her reminded me of every hit I took from Garrett in her name, the pain I endured to live up to her expectations of me. My scars were proof that I was forever changed into the woman she wanted me to be. It was always hard for me to be angry at August, but in that moment I wished anger was the only sentiment I held for her.

"Hello, August," I said coldly. Devin backed away, giving us space to stare across the house at each other. Haden managed to find something of interest to do in the kitchen cupboards, so she didn't interfere with the showdown.

"Hello, Lenore," August said as she strolled over to me. She was offering a little bit of a smile, but I couldn't match it. "How did everything go?"

"Well enough. I'm sure most of the evidence of my work has started to heal, but I assure you the scars remain."

August looked a little hurt, but she smiled anyway. "I hope you understand now why I did this." She moved around me toward the fire.

I wasn't sure if it was Garrett's training, my self-professed psychic ability, or my understanding of August, but I already knew what she was doing.

"Yes, I understand your purpose."

August grabbed the fireplace poker and whipped it at my head. It took everything I had not to block it, especially since I could have kicked it out of her hand before she brought it up to swing. The poker stopped millimeters from my face. August looked crestfallen, but then she realized I hadn't flinched. Her eyes shone bright until she saw the savage glare on my face.

I perked an eyebrow at her. "Shall I dance for you now? Or do you prefer to play with my marionette strings?" August lowered the poker. I saw her glance at Devin. She didn't even know how to handle me. "We've disappointed each other. I haven't lived up to your expectations of me and you certainly haven't lived up to mine. Don't worry, though. I understand what you want now. I can be the person *you* want me to be."

August took the stinging concession like a punch in the gut, but she didn't try to offer anything to make me feel better about being abandoned for three months.

"Well," Devin said, rubbing his hands together behind me. He pressed them down on my shoulders and squeezed like he might be able to release the tension in the room by easing the tension in my shoulders. "How about you start dinner while I tell you all about my feat of bravery?"

"I've already eaten." I pulled away from his hands and sat down in the chair next to the fire to read my latest book. I could tell everyone was baffled by this new change of hierarchy, but no one dared contest it. I had made my stand.

Clemency and Cigarettes

T HE LOOKOUT ROTATION RESUMED normally that night. I took the early shift. Instead of my customary spot on the side porch, I sat on the railing of the back porch in the dark, listening to the cicadas. Unfortunately, the apocalypse hadn't done anything to lessen the insect population.

I decided to take a couple extra hours so Devin didn't take the bulk of the evening himself. He usually took midnight to three o'clock, Haden took three to six, and August was up early. Most nights though, Devin didn't wake Haden and did a full six-hour shift. This in turn prompted August to wake a little earlier to compensate. Haden always griped at him for not waking her, but it was obvious she appreciated it.

Well before two, Devin pulled himself off the couch where he had been napping and joined me. "Hey," he said, still rubbing the sleep from his eyes.

"What are you doing? I told you I'd wake you."

He leaned on the railing beside me and pulled out his pack of cigarettes. He offered me one and I took it. Smoking wasn't really my thing, but it was something to do, and nobody cared about cancer anymore. Slow suicide was back in style.

He lit mine first, as any gentleman would. I sipped a drag off it that made my lungs want to crawl out of my throat and slap me in the face. I managed to only cough a little. He chuckled quietly to himself as he enjoyed a few long drags of his cigarette. He sucked them in like a veteran beer drinker might chug his first can of beer to quench his thirst.

"You okay?" Devin asked, but before I could give him the cliché *fine,* he asked again. "For real, are you okay?"

I flicked my cigarette a few times to make the embers glow before answering. "I'm mad." I looked up at him to see if he was going to hightail and run at the honesty.

"At all of us?" he asked. His face was barely visible, but I knew he could see mine. I could almost picture the worry etched in his beautiful eyes. He wasn't a fighter—at least not socially—he was a lover, and it would grieve him desperately to be the cause of my pain.

"No," I said in all honesty. "For once I'm mad at August."

"She's a hard woman to be mad at."

"I know." I took a drag of my cigarette so it didn't look like I had wasted it. The second time wasn't nearly as bad, but it did bring to mind what it might feel like to suffocate in a burning building.

"Was it tough, the last three months?" he asked.

"Yes." He didn't seem to like that answer. He was probably hoping I would say it got easier each day, or I learned fast, but since the stakes kept getting raised, I didn't really know how far I'd come, until I was there. "The stupid thing is, I spent the last three months learning to be independent from you guys, and I think the only thing I accomplished was becoming dependent on Garrett."

Devin looked away, suddenly preoccupied with something else. It was probably just his reservations against prying, but it also might have been a tinge of jealousy. When he finally turned back, he stepped closer to me and I could see the anger on his face. "He didn't take advantage of you, did he—out here, alone?"

I almost smiled, but decided I needed to take Devin's concerns seriously. "Garrett put me through a lot, but he didn't hurt me like that."

Devin seemed content with that. "I have to tell you about the tournaments." I could hear the excitement in his voice. He was nearly giddy.

I crushed out my cigarette and touched his arm. "Tell me tomorrow, okay?" I gave him a smile that hopefully apologized for not being attentive to the ten-year-old boy inside of him. "Don't stay up all night. The point of a rotation is to share the burden."

I started to climb off the railing, but he grabbed me and lifted me off. After my feet were down, he kept me in a close embrace. "I know you're supposed to be our new secret weapon, but don't change, okay? I liked you the way you were."

I was tempted to ask if that included being his kitchen slave, but I decided not to ruin the generous compliment. "Okay." He pulled me forward and kissed me. It was a long, firm lip press that seemed to express his gratitude, remorse, and relief all in one.

When he let me go, I smiled at him. He didn't smile back, but I got the sense he was still worried about me, despite my agreement not to change. It was probably warranted, but my anger would either dissipate or curdle into something else. In this case, it was probably going to be bitterness.

Population Control

THE SURGE OF COGNIZANT grim was getting on August's nerves. We could barely make it through the center of town to get supplies without a full-on attack. She wanted us to drag some out for target practice. Naturally, I was the bait.

They dropped me off in the center of town, at the highway crossroads. I walked south while the threat was low, but the older grim easily sensed my presence. Like a fork to steak, they were ready to dig in. That left me a little under a mile to sprint to the viaduct. I already had a couple dozen grim to outrun and that was increasing by the second. My training over the last few months made running the distance effortless. However, the rising overpass made my run-for-your-life pace, a little grueling.

I thought the viaduct was a stupid place for the showdown, but I didn't voice my opinion, since I didn't know why I thought that. A strategy four minutes in the planning and twenty minutes in the execution didn't leave much room for constructive criticism.

The crowd of grim hot on my tail were unaffected by my hyperventilating speed. I felt a pull at the back of my shirt, but a well-placed bullet from Haden's side arm took out the cause of it. I was pleased she was as good a shot as she claimed, since my head was among the possible targets.

I rolled over car hoods, to save myself the time it would take to weave through them. I saw my offensive line at the peak of the inclined road. The great thing about the grim was they weren't usually smart. If they had a target in mind, they kept right on coming. Apparently demons didn't understand the concept of retreat.

When I made it past my front line, Devin opened fire from atop his Dodge with his shotgun, and Haden with her pistol. August stayed on the ground and took care of any that made it through with her samurai sword. Haden didn't bother reloading when she ran out. She jumped down with August and went straight to bashing their brains in with a bat.

"Lenore!" August called back to me when Devin couldn't manage to thin the line enough for her comfort.

"Yeah, yeah, I'm coming," I panted as I dug my bow out of the back of the truck. I was tired, sweaty, and I might have pulled a hamstring diving into the truck bed, but once I was lined up, all I needed was arm strength and eyes.

I nocked each arrow, drew, and released as fast as my dexterity allowed. The rapid repetition was impressive, though my aim was probably off a little. I took out nearly a dozen before my arrows ran out. I noted a look of shock from everyone, when they realized I had cleared the entire frontal attack in a matter of seconds. It gave Haden a moment to reload, and August time to rest her arms.

My tickling concern about our strategy was nearly to the fire-ant stage. The intuitive anxiety provided the warning, but no explanation for its cause. So all I could do was be on guard.

I took a moment to gather a few arrows that had spilled from my quiver, so I could avoid resorting to hand-to-hand combat.

As I bent down to pick up my arrows, I saw movement out of the corner of my eye. It was then I realized why the viaduct was such a stupid idea.

I grabbed the tire iron from the floor of the truck bed and flung it near Devin's head. He saw the threat and ducked, though I suspected it would have missed him.

Before he could harangue me about poor sportsmanship in battle, the hiss of the bludgeoned grim behind him announced itself. He whipped around and bashed the remainder of its head in. It slumped over the side of the truck, empty of demon presence.

Devin might have afforded me a glance to thank me, but his eyes were transfixed on the attack coming from the south side of the viaduct. The intelligent portion of the horde had wrapped around beneath the overpass. We were flanked by grim north and south, with no option of east or west without risking broken legs from the four-story drop.

Devin cursed and called to August, but she was preoccupied with another surge on the north. Haden jumped back up on the truck bed with us and pegged off the closest attackers on either side. Devin struggled to get his shotgun loaded. It was a good weapon for multiple attackers, but at some point you had to reload, and then it was a liability. August was right; you couldn't always rely on a weapon to save you. Eventually you would run out of ammunition.

"What the fuck are you doing, Lenore?" Haden yelled at me. "Pick up your damn arrows and help!"

I looked down at the half dozen arrows mixed in with leaves and tools on the floor of the truck. I looked out at the thirty plus grim on the south side and the dozen or so left on the north side. Even with Haden's bullets this would end with hand-to-hand combat.

"Stop shooting, Haden," I said as I reached down for a ball-peen hammer I noticed when searching for arrows.

"What?" Haden said, shooting three more times.

"Devin, go help August clear up the north side and then get the truck started and come save my ass."

"What, where are you—?" Devin protested, trying to grab me before I jumped down.

"Haden, cover me!" I yelled behind me as I ran into the melee of grim. I heard two concurrent cusses followed by a bullet that kept one of the three grim I was approaching from ripping off my arm while I kicked and hit the other two.

One hit with the hammer and a grim would go down with a shattered skull, but getting the hammer there was the problem. I raised it high, only to get my wrist lassoed. I flipped the offending hijacker over my back with strength I didn't actually have—but that's why God gave us adrenaline. A favor, but not a savior.

I struggled to get free from the grim's unrelenting grip while Haden shot the ones trying to take advantage of my leashed position. I gave up trying to pry at his fingers and broke his arm off at the elbow with my foot. The satisfying crack was reminiscent of breaking up pallets for the winter fire.

I dragged the half arm along with me, bitch-slapping a few grim with it as I climbed to the top of a hybrid SUV. In the elevated position,

I kicked and hammered in the heads of the aggressors scrambling to rise with me.

Across my sea of predictable attackers, I saw a grim ascend to the top of a minivan. He looked at me with intelligent eyes that were creepy as hell. I couldn't help smiling at his sidelong, double-dog-daring stare. All he needed was a long jet-black coat flapping in the wind behind him and I might have swooned from his romantic villain portrayal.

"I'm out, Lenore!" Haden yelled at me, warning me that she was no longer going to be able to save me. I stomped my foot, shattering the hand that was trying to trip me. I should have been paying closer attention to the rat bastards at my feet, but I got the feeling my dark-eyed friend across the way was far more dangerous than all of them combined.

I heard August yell at me from the expanse of cars separating us, but I also felt the words penetrating through my mind, demanding my retreat. Her superhero psychic link to danger was screaming to save me, but she couldn't get to me. It was damned ironic that the one time I was standing my ground and fighting, she was begging me to run for my life.

I smashed another set of fingers and kicked a face, but I never took my eyes off the former man across from me. When he saw my intention was to fight him, he opened his mouth and roared with an inhuman voice. The other grim seemed to rally with this call to war—as if the pandemonium currently surrounding me wasn't enough to incite their hellish dispositions.

I found his attempt to frighten me with boogeyman tactics infuriating, to say the least. I had just spent three months being beaten to a pulp by a man I might have accidentally fallen in love with. I wasn't about to let a loud-mouthed demon get the better of me with a stereo voice-over from hell.

I took in a deep breath and half yelled, half screamed back at him. The cathartic scream came out better than I intended, and the grim, including *Captain Kick My Ass*, stopped to stare at me. I laughed at his dumbfounded look. Apparently he wasn't used to women who spoke their mind.

I shifted in preparation for my mano-a-mano duel, but August's arm came out of nowhere and latched around me. We fell back into the truck bed together. The Dodge's tires squealed as Devin peeled out. Haden kicked out a few grim that were applying for stowaway status.

I watched my newfound arch-enemy shrink into the distance, along with all of his vermin friends. I almost hated leaving, because I wanted to see how that fight would have turned out.

Reality Check

"**W**HAT THE FUCK WAS that?" Haden asked once we were free of the direct onslaught of grim.

"That was the new me," I said, pulling away from August's protective embrace.

"Really? Getting yourself killed is the new you?" Haden yelled. She was precariously standing through Devin's driving, but I knew she wouldn't give up her lording position to sit down and scold me. Her hands were propped on her hips, and she was panting from her exhaustive efforts to clear a path through the grim so August could, once again, save me. Her jaw was clenched tight, but it wasn't anger I saw behind her narrowed eyes, it was concern.

I missed most of the lead-up to my rescue, but I imagine from their perspective I was on the verge of being overtaken by a massive swarm of demon-propelled bad guys, via the instruction of the kingpin. They must have been tripping over themselves trying to get coordinated to save my ostensibly suicidal ass. Until that moment, I had no idea how much my friends would be willing to risk to save my life.

I looked back at August, who had the same agitation on her face. She couldn't bring herself to look at me. She no doubt blamed herself for my eagerness to prove my worth. "I wasn't trying to kill myself, Haden."

"You could've fucking fooled me!" she griped before settling herself in for the ride.

"I'm sorry," I apologized to the back of her head. "I didn't mean to put you in danger. I was trying to save you."

"You did," August said meekly. "The grim left us alone and swarmed around you. We could have left you behind and saved ourselves." I looked at her with a question on my face that didn't need to be asked, but I couldn't help but think it. She stared at me, finding the mettle to meet me eye to eye. "Never," she said firmly, answering my unspoken question. "I would never let you sacrifice yourself for us. You're too..." She trailed off, but I got the gist of her you-are-so-beautiful-to-me speech.

When Haden finally looked at me, she was back to her usual angry self. "What was that back there anyway? It looked like you were enjoying yourself." I shrugged, not wanting to admit how much I wanted to go back to the viaduct and finish my fight. "You do realize that grim could have snapped your neck with one hand?" she continued to lecture me. "Those old fuckers are fast."

I nodded, but I wasn't sure I agreed. He was obviously going to be a handful, but something told me I might have gotten the better of him. I didn't know why my ego had flared so brightly where he was concerned, but I wasn't going to overanalyze it.

After a few minutes of silence, Haden moved between us and poked her head into the cab. "I want a beer!" she demanded, and Devin immediately started to decelerate to turn around and find a safe bar.

Real Folk

MY TOWN WASN'T TOTALLY devoid of life. After all, I wasn't the only heretic born and raised in the town that Wal-Mart killed. The few that were left, had either gone into hiding and were living off the land, or embraced their lack of greater purpose like early retirement. Within the latter group were the barflies.

Drinking was a pastime my hometown was known for. More bars than churches wasn't just a matter of priority; it was necessity. Aside from praying on Sundays and bowling on Tuesdays, there was nothing to do in this stinking town but drink.

Naturally, the bar crowd was mostly alcoholics who had no concern for their livers. Since the town hadn't run dry yet, there was no reason for them to sober up if they didn't want to.

Devin's preferred watering hole was the Double T. He found the name intrinsically humorous. He entered first, drawing the first few glares and guns from the patrons inside. No one was intentionally unfriendly. It was just instinct. Although, I'm not sure that could be blamed on the apocalypse. It might have been a lack of social grace created by a population with higher morals than standards.

Once the grouches and grousers had settled back down and holstered their weapons, Devin manned the bar for us. He brought us each a beer, popping the top on each one like he was familiar with the sticky side of a counter. "Ladies," he leaned over the bar and tapped his beer to each of ours, "to being back in the *bosom*," he winked at me, "of our family. May we never need to separate again."

"Hear, hear!" Haden raised her beer before chugging it down in an impromptu contest with Devin.

I looked past Haden to offer August a nod before drinking my beer. At least a small gesture so she knew I was glad they were back, even if I wasn't the same woman I was when they left me.

Her face was somber and distant, probably pressured by a great number of things on her mind. I imagined she was still dwelling on my almost demise, but it seemed to be something more internal than her usual motherly concerns. I wanted to know what her troubles were, but when my mouth opened, I poured beer into it.

Beer Shot with an Adrenaline Chaser

H ADEN SHOUTED MORE THAN sang with the music blasting out of the truck's rear window. I offered a quick retort to her bridge when she shoved her imaginary microphone in my face. I was always willing to play along with Haden's playful drunk side. It was her hungover side I avoided.

The sun was nearly gone, but the twilight lingering in the sky was enough to light our way home. Instead of joining the concert in back, August opted to sit in the cab. She was slumped against the passenger door across from Devin, pondering her woes in silence. I still wanted to ask her what was wrong, but I hadn't decided if I wanted the answer.

I crawled over and stuck my head in the window. "Hey." Devin turned down the music so he could hear me. "Stop by the church, I need to see Priest."

Devin immediately glanced at August for permission. She looked at me with the same concern everyone held for me when I mentioned Priest.

"What for?" August asked as if she was only curious and not searching for a way to dissuade me.

"I haven't seen him in months, I'd like to let him know I'm alive, and not... in training anymore." *Being beaten to a pulp* was what I wanted to say, but I was making a concerted effort not to be a bitch. A brat yes, but not a bitch.

"I don't know if that's such a good idea. It's getting late," August said half-heartedly.

"Yeah, that's why I want to stop now, rather than go back with the four-wheeler in the dead of night." I tipped my brow, challenging her to choose between the options.

"You won't be long, will you?" she asked.

"You won't even need to shut the engine off. I just want to update him. Assuming he's not with his harem, I'll be five minutes. If he is, then no minutes, we'll go home."

August nodded to Devin and he made the next turn to head to the small white church on the gravel backroads. As I pulled my head back, Haden jabbed my shoulder—painfully, but she didn't know that.

"Why'd we turn? Where are we going?"

"To see Priest. It won't take long."

Haden grimaced at me. It wasn't the worried look she had earlier, but still her condescending version of it. "What do you see in him?"

I paused to think about my answer. "Pain, usually," I said before sitting back against the cab. Haden lost the severity of the disdain in her eyes and didn't say anything more on the topic.

When the truck pulled into the drive, I hopped out. I ran to the front doors of the church prepared for a fly-by "Hi." I couldn't hear anything over the truck engine so I peered inside. There was no evidence of carnal activities, so I slipped through the doors.

The flickering candlelight was no longer coming from the red wall sconces, but from a mixture of various wax candles around the church.

The collection apparently included some scented ones, because the church smelled like Halloween threw up on Christmas.

I stopped midway down the aisle. "Priest." I waited to see if he was inside his dressing room, but I didn't hear him stir. "Priest!" I raised my voice to unmistakable decibels in case he was too trashed to tell the difference between me and his hallucinations.

I felt something was off more than knew. Like the shiver you get when you aren't cold or the one hiccup with none to follow. Something wasn't right.

I turned back just as August approached. She seemed surprised that I sensed her, but I wasn't sure I had. I would take credit for the coincidence though.

"What's wrong?" she asked, surveying the room.

"What? I don't know—nothing... something. He's not here. He's always here."

"Behind the altar." August nodded to the front of the church.

I looked it over. I saw nothing but a slew of drug paraphernalia littered on the sacred table. When I lowered my focus, I saw his feet sticking out from behind it. "Priest?" I was asking myself, not calling to him.

Once I was sure something was wrong, my feet moved. I rounded the marble table and found Priest on the floor. His eyes were narrow slits and his face was ghostly pale. A trail of residual vomit tracked down his cheeks. It was a movie scene I never anticipated seeing in real life.

"Shit!" I hissed and dove to his side. "Priest!" I checked him for signs of life. He was breathing shallowly and his pulse was weak. "Priest!" I yelled at him and slapped his cheek.

"Lenore," August said softly behind me.

"No, August, he's alive," I said.

"I know, but..." She trailed off and I looked back at her. "There's nothing you can do for him. Either he'll make it or he won't."

I narrowed my eyes at her. "Can't we... adrenaline shot!" I blurted out my feeble movie-learned first aid.

"No, that's not going to help. His heart isn't in trouble, it's his lungs."

"A cold shower to shock him awake?"

"No." August shook her head again somberly. "There's no more 911, Lenore. There's common sense and antibiotics. That's it. Let him be, and I'll check on him tomorrow."

"No." I shook my head. "What if he dies?"

"He'll die either way, or he'll live either way."

I looked down at Priest's pale face. I got the feeling this was intentional. If God wouldn't invite him, he would crash the party. "Then he'll die or live with me by his side."

"Lenore, he could be out for hours or days. Please don't ask me to leave you here."

"Fine, then let's take him with us," I negotiated.

August sighed and knelt beside me. Her eyes were more sympathetic and supportive than I expected. She really did love me. And as angry as I still was, I loved her too. I could barely meet her gaze, because I knew if she asked me to, I would leave with her.

"I wanted to save you this pain. I didn't want you to have to watch him die like... this," she said, correcting whatever she initially intended to end with.

"I know." I nodded. "I'm a sucker for lost causes. I used to bring stray cats home by the litter. Drove my mom nuts." I chuckled at thinking how similar the situation was. Only, Priest wasn't a stray, he was mine. My friend. I couldn't leave him here to die. "Wouldn't he have a better chance with a warm fire and a slap in the face every couple hours?"

"And what if he doesn't survive?" she asked.

My eyes watered and danced over hers. I smiled and shrugged. "I never got to keep the cats either."

She looked down at Priest. I could see the disgust she still felt for him. The same disgust I used to feel when I looked at him. "Are you sure he wants to be saved?"

"I know he doesn't." She looked at me, questioning where my motivation was coming from. "We're the heroes, right?"

She put her hand firmly on my shoulder. "Just once though, okay? I won't have you spending your post-apocalyptic life caring for a man who doesn't care about himself." I nodded, but she shook my shoulder to get a more affirmative answer.

"I'll save him once. After that, he's on his own."

It still sounded strange, putting limitations on my heroism. I couldn't imagine Superman handing out punch cards for rescues. Only one rescue per year and ten total per lifetime. At any rate, I understood what she meant. To her, Priest was beyond hope, destined to be among the "day tens."

Satisfied with my resolve—to limit my resolve—August and I loaded Priest up and took him back to the house.

Overnight Guest

"L IKE THIS?" I ASKED August for the third time.

"Not so hard. You're just stimulating with pain, not trying to bruise him.

I eased the pressure of my knuckles on Priest's sternum as I rubbed them up and down his chest. "Is this all I can do?"

"If he starts to stir, try to wake him up. Conscious is always better. If he stops breathing, resuscitate. Keep his airways clear and..." August chuckled. "...Pray."

I rolled my eyes at the irony before responding. "I'm sorry to put you in this position. I know you'd rather he just die."

August frowned. "I care about you. I don't want him to hurt you. By that reasoning, I want him to live, very much."

"Thank you."

August left me alone to tend to my patient by the light of the living room fire. Sheets and blankets had been laid down to protect the carpet from any unintentional body functions, upper or lower. Without much to do but play nursemaid to a coma victim, I cleaned him up.

I washed the vomit from his face, and put drops in his half-lidded eyes to keep them moist. In a perhaps fruitless effort to encourage breathing, I removed his clergy collar and unbuttoned his shirt. I couldn't help but touch his chest to feel his inhalations and heartbeat against my hand. Despite the joke, I did offer a silent prayer that was more an observation than a plea.

You didn't want him before. Why take him now?

After repeated efforts to wake him, I finally gave up and settled in for the night beside him. Close enough to hear his slow breaths. Throughout the night, I woke to him rousing, but he was out again too fast to bother doing anything else.

The next morning, he was still alive, and that was the only improvement, aside from not having to clean up vomit. The sun wasn't up yet, but Haden came in off her post. She looked over the scene of me sprawled beside Priest fretting about respiration, brain damage, and other such things I didn't understand.

"I can watch him. Get some air," she commanded.

I shook my head. "I know you guys don't care about him. I don't expect you to help him."

"I don't, but I'm not offering to help him, I'm offering to help you. I'm running on three hours of sleep, and you still look less rested than me."

I almost smiled at her for the joke, but I could tell from the dryness in my throat and eyes that I probably looked worn down. I nodded and pushed myself up off the floor, regaining most of my bipedal mammal status. I grabbed Priest's clergy collar off the fireplace mantel and I headed outside to bathe my worries in fresh air.

Haden grabbed my arm before I hit the door. It wasn't gentle, but as usual, she didn't know that. "You know he can't save you, don't you?"

She didn't mean my life. Her eyes were stern, begging me to protect myself.

"I know," I whispered. "But there's still a chance I can save him." I didn't mean his life either.

Day Tens

T EN DAYS.

That's how long it took to come to terms with the post-apocalyptic world. I mentioned I spent three months immersed in self-pity, doubt, shame, and loneliness, before I reconciled with my fate. But the first ten days were still the hardest.

I may have given a playfully satiric description of day one, but allow me to rein in any humor and once again express that, one minute, I was a hard-working, under-paid grocery clerk. The next, I was standing in a sea of dead bodies.

The formula for that conversation in your brain goes something like this. *This can't be happening. Why is this happening? What do I do? Please, God no! Please, God NO! PLEASE, GOD NO!* If you reciprocate the integer times ten to the 100th power, you begin to form a picture of my thought processes taking place over the first 48 hours.

This is key, because within that first 48 hours, everyone on Earth was thinking the same thing. Even the greatest of tragedies pale in comparison to the electric spine-tingling psychic energy that was produced by this event. It was within those first two days that everyone knew, without abjuration, *the truth*.

He was there.

And we were not in His good graces.

Into day three, the electric energy of thousands upon thousands of collective thoughts faded away. We started to think about survival. Panic set in fast, but it quickly eroded when we realized the demand for food and water was at an all-time low.

On day four people started vandalizing, either in anger or because they could. It's a strange desire, but somewhere in our human DNA is a gene that insists when the world goes to pot, we must break glass and spray-paint profanities on walls.

Day five, the anger fades, because you realize no one is going to punish you. Just to the left of the vandalism gene is the gene that creates our desire for punishment. Technically the gene should be on the right, but what can you do.

Day six is when you start to feel the emptiness. That's when you realize you aren't going to wake up. It's not a dream.

Day seven and you've reached a week. This should be the transitional day, but it's not. You become numb. Everything that's happening is happening. That's all the farther you get with that pseudo-philosophical thought process. It's real.

Day eight, you're depressed. It goes without saying, but there is something horrifying about turning the calendar back to that dreaded day of the week for the first time.

Day nine, you're angry again. It doesn't matter at whom and the point is moot. You just can't stand that all of it has been left on your shoulders to figure out, to survive, to atone.

Damn Him.

Day ten.

It takes ten days to realize you just came full circle, and you are about to repeat it again: atonement, loneliness, numbness, sorrow, anger. Rinse and repeat.

Day ten was when the second wave of bodies arrived. They didn't receive the astounding shock value that the millions received, but to those remaining, the death of even one more person near them was intolerable. Incidentally, those who die after the apocalypse don't crystallize. They rot where they lay.

The day ten suicides were a lesson, a warning, and an answer to a question no one wanted to ask. *What's going to happen to me when I die?*

Priest should have been a day ten suicide. I wasn't sure if he didn't want to die or if he just didn't want to piss off God *that much*. Either way, he had made it over a year without *accidentally* overdosing. I wasn't about to let him give up now.

You're WELCOME!

"**Y**OU HAD NO RIGHT to interfere!"

Priest's finger was nearly mining my nose with its proximity. I should have expected him to be mad. His slow recovery over the last three days was littered with glares, snarls, and not-so-witty insults about my personal faults. None of which bothered me, since he didn't know enough about me to hurt my feelings too deeply.

"You were dying!" I yelled back, nearly ready to bite his finger off.

My back was pinned to the stove. I was in the process of making him some cream of wheat for breakfast when I made the mistake of opening the can of worms marked: *What's wrong?* Traditionally men don't share their feelings, but given that Priest had no intention of rising on the third day, he had a lot to say to me.

"Why were you even there?" He pulled his finger back and ripped at his hair. The glossy black mess was freshly cleaned, but it still looked like he had recently applied a hot oil treatment.

"To let you know my training was done! In case you were worried about me!"

"You should have left me there! How dare you interfere with God's will?"

"Overdosing is not God's will!"

"It is if he tells me to take it!"

"Jesus Christ, Priest, how nuts are you?" I hadn't expected him to slap me. I expected a lot of bluster and blow from him, but I didn't expect that. By the look I saw on his face after I recovered, neither did he.

"Oh, Lenore—" was all he got out before Devin tackled him to the floor.

"Damn it! Don't hurt him, Devin! I just put him back together!" I complained as I pulled at Devin's shoulder.

"He hit you!" Devin looked back at me, appalled by my casual attitude toward the abuse.

"No, he slapped me, and not even that hard." I squeezed his shoulder instead of pulling him. It seemed to draw him back more than my strength. "Besides, I'm on a first name basis with both Garrett's fists; I don't think one little slap is going to break me now."

Devin's eyes softened. He still didn't understand what had happened to me the last three months. He didn't need to. He didn't want to.

"What's going on here?" August came in from her sunrise watch.

"Nothing I can't handle," I said firmly, giving her a look that said *stay out of it.*

"Your breakfast is boiling over." She nodded to the stove.

"Son of a bitch!" I growled, tending to the mess on the stove. I could sense August smiling at me before I even looked at her. I narrowed my eyes at her even though my lips were starting to curl to mirror her. "What?"

"You cuss a lot more now," she said with a bigger smile.

I wasn't sure how to react to that. Her tone was complimentary. She seemed to be implying that my crassness was directly related to my confidence. If that was the case, I was very confident lately. "Shut up," I said when I couldn't think of a clever response. I had to look away from her, because I couldn't contain my smile.

Satisfied with the scene as such, and me in a state of flushed amusement, she headed upstairs. Behind me Devin had moved Priest to a chair and was brandishing his finger at him like Priest had only moments ago done to me. Devin's voice was too low for me to hear over the stove vent I had turned on, but from the look on Priest's face, he was no doubt discovering how thick Devin's chivalrous streak was. Priest nodded at him abjectly.

Devin turned around cracking his neck. I smiled, wondering if I should swoon so he could catch me too. He stopped before me and gently touched my cheek, as if he could undo the trauma of it all with his sweetness. His eye caught on something at my forehead and he shifted uncomfortably before plastering a smile on his face. He gave me a wet good morning kiss and shuffled off to give Priest and me privacy to continue arguing.

I instinctively touched the area his eyes had caught on. A scar under my hairline, long and ugly. I was thankful it was there and not across my face. Garrett was just happy I had blocked him at the last second, since he would have split my skull. Not that the gash didn't bleed bad enough for us to be concerned about that.

It was one of many scars Devin hadn't seen or noticed. My three months in training were no joke, which was why Priest's slap was more irritating than traumatizing. But once again, Devin didn't need to know all that. His knight in shining armor side would be outraged, and it would eat him alive to know he walked away so it could happen.

"Lenore," Priest said meekly.

"Oh, shit," I griped and turned back to the cream of wheat that had magically bubbled to near explosion again. "I was making enough for both of us, but this is only enough for one now." I turned back and Priest was right behind me. "Sit down!" I hadn't meant to say it so fiercely, but his presence had startled me and my only options were to yell or throw the mush on him. I never was much for wasting food.

Priest backpedaled with his hands up in surrender. "Okay, okay." He sat down, placing his hands on the table flat like I might suspect he had a weapon otherwise. He watched me spoon the mush into a bowl and add an excess of honey and a little evaporated milk. Just a dash of cinnamon and I was pleased to offer my favorite childhood breakfast to him.

I slid the bowl across the table with a spoon stuck in it. He caught the dish, but kept his eyes on me. I sat down and waited for him to take a bite. His eyes melted into a flurry of desperate remorse. I already knew what he was going to say before he said it. "Lenore—"

"Shut up," I said, not wanting to hear the apology. It was written on his face the minute he did it. The sentiment in his eyes meant more to me than words. "Take a bite." He looked down at the unappetizing mush and dug the spoon in for a big bite. "Not like that, you heathen." I smirked. "Slowly. Let the texture be forgiven by the milk, and let the cinnamon whisper over the honey."

He offered me a thin smile. He was trying to match my mood, but he still looked dejected. He took the bite, closing his eyes as he had taught me with the strawberries. I smiled, watching him. It was probably a running joke among priests that if you couldn't have sex, at least you could have food.

When he opened his eyes, I could see a little of his agony had been eased.

"There," I said proudly. "Aren't you at least glad for that little Earthly delight?"

"Lenore—"

"Shush. Just eat. You need your strength. August doesn't let me keep strays." I winked. He narrowed his eyes, dubious of either my comment or my wink, I wasn't sure which. "I'm going upstairs to shower. Someone has kept me too busy to shave my legs and you know how women hate to miss shaving." His lip twisted in a smirk, but he didn't speak. "I trust I don't need to hide the steak knives." I said it like a joke but I raised my brow and waited for an answer.

"Thank you for the... breakfast," he said, stumbling over the definition of the sludge I was making him eat.

"It's cream of wheat, and if you don't like it—you lie to me and eat it anyway because I don't waste my favorite food on just anyone." I noted that he hadn't answered my question. "Priest..."

"I'm fine. I love the cream of wheat. I'm honored to be among the few you would offer it to. Go shave your legs." He nodded dismissively and I felt a tinge of guilt.

I wondered if he really did want to die. Maybe he was right about God's will. Maybe He just forgot him, and had planned to pick him up later. Conversely though, I couldn't help but notice his suicidal overdose landed on the night after August came back. Any night before that and I wouldn't have been there. Wasn't that God's will too?

The Act of Appreciation

S INCE STRAYS WERE NOT welcome, I did my best to feed my rehabilitated pet in the hopes that he might make it on his own in the wild. Unfortunately, his days without drugs were making his stomach reject anything that didn't make him high. The trembling that set in was a little scary, but August assured me it was a good thing. It meant everything was officially out of his system.

Being sober wasn't something Priest was good at anymore, and the mood swings were enough to make August demand he finish his recovery at his church. Despite my misgivings about returning him to the home of his vices, I knew his sobriety wasn't strictly contingent on his location.

I jumped out of the driver's side of the truck and jogged around to the passenger's side to help him out, but he waved me off with a shaking hand. "I'm a drug addict, not a cripple."

"I know. That's why I'm trying to help. A cripple would be able to function on his own." He glared at me, but the smile I wore left him defenseless. It was funny and he knew it.

"Will you walk me in?" he requested and reached out his hand. I wasn't entirely sure what to do with it, so when I didn't respond to it, he let it drop. "I'm so sorry, Lenore."

"Oh, please don't start apologizing for that now."

"I wasn't. I will and I am, but I'm apologizing now for not being thankful for your rescue. You are a *good* person. I shouldn't have made you feel bad for saving me."

"I don't feel bad for saving you," I corrected immediately. "You are a *good* person too."

He looked down at his shaking hands and shook his head. "I'm fallen, Lenore. I have disgraced God. I have degraded my title."

"Okay, first off, I think fallen only gets to be used for people in love, or angels—and..." I looked behind him for wings. "I don't think you're one of those. Second, you haven't done anything new. It may be new to you, but guess what, sex, drugs, and strawberry fields have been around long before you discovered them."

"But my thoughts, my anger. You have no idea the things I have done to ridicule my creator."

I smiled. "I'm sure I've accidentally walked in on some of them. Kudos for your stamina, by the way; pent-up celibacy apparently works better than Viagra." He flushed at the comment. "My point is, none of that matters, because you're not a priest anymore." I flicked his freshly laundered black shirt he insisted on buttoning to the strangulation level.

His eyes narrowed, and I thought for a moment he was mad, but he smirked at me. "Have I seriously been too stoned to remember your sharp tongue or has your training changed you that much?"

I shrugged, taking on the blush this time. "It's all me... and maybe a little of the training. At any rate, I'm just more of me than I was before. A better version of me. Lenore 2.0."

Priest nodded. "I like it." He paused, looking me over. "I wish I could be a better version of myself."

I took his hand in mine, and he looked down at it like I had stuck a snake in his hand. "Come on, cripple man. Let's get you situated," I said as I dragged him inside the church.

The Act of Depreciation

THERE WAS A SMALL moment of awkwardness when it was time to let go of his hand. I didn't know how to do it, since I was the one who had instigated it. Priest must have sensed my discomfort and squeezed my hand before releasing me.

The candles had since snubbed out, leaving the church dimly lit by the stained-glass windows. The semi-pleasant holiday smell now took the backseat to the lingering smell of vomit. I frowned and looked at him. "Are you sure you can't stay in the rectory?"

He shook his head. I didn't bother arguing. I knew he liked to stay in the church to wallow in his misery. I had hoped his sober mind might see things differently, but apparently not.

"You've seriously got to give this place up, Priest. It's killing you—obviously. You're not..." I motioned to the room, "...this anymore."

"Yes, you mentioned I'm not a priest anymore, but what you fail to understand is that I can't just take off my collar and magically become a different man. Speaking of my collar, where is it?" He pinned an accusing gaze on me.

"I have it, but you aren't going to wear it anymore." I pulled the collar from my cleavage. I didn't want it to crease it in my pocket. He eyed the sudden appearance and grabbed for it. I pulled it behind my back and to my surprise he continued to press the issue. "Back off!" He stopped reaching for it, but the glower he was giving me made me wonder if he might get physical with me again.

"Give it to me, now!" he seethed. "It's the only one I have left."

"I'll keep it safe for you, but you aren't wearing it anymore."

"How dare you!"

"How dare *you*!" I screeched. "You stopped being a priest the minute you sidled up next to the seven deadly sins. Wearing this isn't a statement, it's just another addiction."

He lunged for the collar, grabbing my arm to hold it while he reached around me to grab it. I grabbed his reaching arm with my free hand, leaving me in a pinned-back embrace with him. "Priest, I don't doubt you'll be able to get it from me, but rest assured the last three months have given me the skills to take it back again."

He must have been surprised by the confidence in my voice, because he stopped to see if I was bluffing or not. I wasn't. And to prove it...

"I've developed a significant pain tolerance during that time as well." I raised my knee slowly up his leg and rested it in his groin. He glanced down at the movement, which was no doubt intriguing in the slow version. "Shall we find out what your tolerance is?"

His face was inches from mine, but we couldn't have been farther apart. I was the mean parent taking away his security blanket. He recovered from his anger and released my arm, but his face was still pinched in a pout as he walked away from me.

"I have something else for you to wear." He stopped and looked back. "If you want it? I made it myself, so it's a little kindergarten pasta art-ish, but I think it might fill the space without being a complete blasphemy to your new hobbies."

"Since when do you care about that?" he asked. He groaned as he gingerly sat down in the front pew. He must have been sore everywhere. Almost dying took a lot out of him.

"I'm not sure I do, but everybody has to draw a line in the sand and this is mine."

"A collar is your line in the sand?" He rubbed his eyes.

"No, you torturing yourself is my line. I can't take it anymore." I joined him in the pew.

"Then why do you keep coming here then?"

I looked away from him. I couldn't help but feel a little sting from that statement after everything I'd done. "Well, someone led me to believe we were friends," I said as acridly as I could to hide my hurt. I may have taken it too far in the opposite direction because he stared at me, waiting for me to look back at him. When I did, he offered me a scolding frown.

"We are friends. I didn't mean now. I meant before. I understand why you came here in the first place, but why did you keep coming back. There are easier ways to deal with the grim." I wanted to mention our code of ethics concerning the home owners, but I knew that was only part of the truth. "Or were you content to watch one of God's own defile himself repeatedly when you didn't consider him a friend?" His snappish tone was starting to irritate me as much as it had August, but I decided the best defense against his mood swings was a good offense.

"I'm pretty sure you weren't the only one being defiled in here." I nodded to the altar. "But if it makes you feel any better, I stopped viewing you as one of God's own the minute I walked into this church the first time and saw you."

His eyes widened and his upper lip nearly lifted into a snarl.

"I could do this all day, Priest," I continued when he didn't offer a retort. "Your nerves are broadcasted in technicolor. I guarantee I can rip you off that high horse you keep climbing back onto." I waved his collar at him. "You didn't fall, you pretentious bastard, you tripped. We all did. Welcome to how the other half lives. The only difference between you and me is I'm strong enough to get off the fucking ground."

"Do you really want to compare a man of faith being left behind, to..." his voice trailed off.

"To what? What were you about to say? Say it! No reason to start holding punches now."

"I was going to say an atheist," he grumbled.

I scoffed and laughed a little. "Oh, I thought you were going to call me a whore or something, which, by the way, I'm not." I paused, wondering what his definition of a whore would be, but let it go, since my definition should have been all that mattered. "Anyway, I'm not an atheist either."

His eyes darted to mine. "Not now, you mean?"

"Not before either. I didn't believe in the principles guiding religion as a political purpose instead of an individual prerogative, but yes, I am, and always have been, part of the mustard seed club."

Priest came at me so fast I almost defended myself. At the last second, I surmised he was going to kiss me and stopped, which was a little surprising to me. However, he did neither. His hands cupped my face and he pressed his forehead to mine and whispered some fandangled Latin crap. I relaxed and let him do his blessing as he saw fit.

When he moved away, I couldn't help but smile.

"What's so funny? I can still bless you. I told you I can't simply hang up who I am."

I smirked, wondering if I should tell him I might have preferred the kiss over the blessing, but decided I didn't even want to admit that to myself.

"I know, Priest." I rubbed my face where he had touched me, to rid myself of any thoughts about him before they manifested into something more. As I pulled my hands through my hair, my near skull crack must have revealed itself. I really needed to start parting my hair differently.

"How did you...?" His eyes ballooned as if he suddenly understood what I meant about being resistant to pain. His jaw dropped and I think if Garrett had been there at that moment, he would have added murder to his list of broken commandments. As it was, his hands balled into fists, making the knuckles go white.

Then all at once he was calm again. He reached over to me again, and I rolled my eyes at the impending blessing. Instead, this time he kissed my cheek. "I'm so sorry, Lenore," he whispered while my ear was still near his lips. He pulled back and caressed my cheek with his thumb. "Please forgive me. I'm so... no, there is no excuse. I will never raise my hand to you again, and, God forbid, when I do, I will cut it off."

It should have been a beautiful sentiment, but it made me smile. "It's okay, Priest. I should have known better than to sully the Lord's name to a sobering priest. Apocalypse or no, you have to draw a line somewhere too."

His face turned ashen and he took in a deep breath. "I didn't slap you for the vanity, Lenore. I slapped you for calling me nuts." His eyes danced over mine and I could sense a certain shame in what he was saying, but at the same time, his resolve to defend his sanity was barely beaten by his determination not to hurt me again.

I took in a deep breath and touched his cheek the way he had touched mine. "Okay, Priest, I won't ever call you crazy again, if..." I dug in my pocket and pulled out a small box that might have held earrings at one time. "If you wear my ugly noddle art instead of your white trim." To my relief he smiled.

The act of Submission

I NEGOTIATED HIS CLERGY collar back into my bra, which Priest watched with mild amusement. I shrugged. "It's safe in there."

"Yes, I would feel safe if..." He let his sentence trail off and shook his head. He didn't want to finish that teasing statement any more than I wanted to joke about him kissing me. It was best to keep the below-the-belt stuff for our arguments. "Thank you."

"Don't thank me yet, you haven't seen my crude attempt at jewelry crafting." I slid over to him to show him the necklace I made for him while he was recovering. "I took some liberties with the crucifixion theme. I hope that isn't insulting to you."

I raised the brown bootlace out of the box, a little embarrassed. I was certain a silver necklace from one of the local jewelry stores would have been less prosaic, but I didn't have the time, and I was already on the theme of shabby-crappy.

The pendant was a folded nail that latched onto the lace by the bent nail head. I dulled the end so it didn't scratch. The horizontal line to my cross was another nail, bent and hammered into oblivion. With Devin's help, I had managed to solder a piece of barbed wire across it. Again, I dulled the points so I wasn't offering tetanus on a platter, but they were still pretty sharp. I debated on spray paint, but the rusted barb and silver nails, looked pretty good together.

I explained my creation and credited Devin for his help. Priest stared at the necklace without a single word to say, or any expression of noteworthy translation. I chuckled and dropped my hand to my lap along with the necklace. "It's okay. You don't have to wear it. It was a lame attempt at pacification."

Before I could deposit it back in the box, he grabbed my hand and took it from me, all the while watching me. I furrowed my brow when he didn't respond. Not a *thank you,* or a smile or even a scowl. His eyes skirted my head like I might have a brain sucker attached to it. "Priest, you don't have to." I reached for it, but he drew his hand away.

"Why do you still call me Priest if you insist I'm not one?" He held up the necklace. "Why do you deny me my collar and yet offer me a beautiful necklace signifying Christ's sacrifice to us?"

I laughed. "I think you're taking liberties with that adjective. I only meant for you to wear it as a reminder that you're not the only believer to have a bad day." I rubbed each of my wrists and hung my hands to mime hanging from a cross. I hissed and mouthed *"ouch"* to him.

His brow furrowed as he laughed at me. He drew his arm behind me on the pew but didn't necessarily touch me; he just wanted a better angle. "I feel like I'm meeting you for the first time. I know I was drugged up, but I don't remember this side of you."

"Perhaps it was because you were drugged up that I wasn't so jovial." He smirked at me and under the scrutiny of a sober Priest I couldn't hold his gaze. "Give me that." I reached for the necklace again, but he tucked it behind his back. "I feel stupid asking you to wear it now."

"I would sooner wear this prouder than my own skin."

I stopped trying to grab the necklace and looked at him with the same befuddlement he had been offering me. "Is that good?" I asked.

He nodded somberly, letting his eyes close as he did. "It means," he said, pinning me with his gaze when he opened them again, "I am prouder wearing this necklace from you than I am of the body my creator gave me." He paused and took in a sudden inhalation of epiphany. "However, I suppose I still have to give Him credit for creating the woman that created the necklace."

"Do you mind if we stop talking about Him?" I asked even as his hand started to brush back my hair. He stopped and nodded, letting his hand fall away.

"Sorry, occupational hazard."

"I know, but you need to refocus your attention on you, not Him. Your thoughts. Your feelings. I hate to bring this up, but I need to ask you to do one more thing for me."

"What's that?"

"I need you to not kill yourself," I said blankly. He raised his brow, but didn't say anything. "I know you're hurting and I don't mean to prolong a life that is in such agony, but you told me we were friends."

"We are."

"I know, but I thought you meant acquaintances or even neighbors. When I saw you lying behind the altar nearly dead, I knew we were *friend* friends. Count-on-each-other friends. Not just can-I-borrow-a-cup-of-holy-water friends."

"I guess I never distinguished, but I see your point."

"Anyway, that really sucked. So, I would like you to consider your second chance at life as a debt to me. I expect you to uphold your part of the bargain by staying alive." He raised his hand, gently touching my face with his two fingers that weren't wrapped around the necklace. He mumbled another Latin ditty. "Priest, please stop blessing me. I feel like every last favor you have left is being used up on me instead of yourself."

I pulled his hand down and held it away from my face. "I don't want you to give me strength to live without you. I want you to be strong enough to live. Here." I wrapped his fingers tightly around the necklace. "Bless this. Put every last honest uncorrupted hope for the future of mankind into a super-whammy blessing." He paused and I squeezed his hand tighter. "Go on. It's not self-serving I'm asking for it."

He closed his eyes and recited a long chant. I waited patiently. He spoke whispers of foreign words for nearly a full minute before he opened his eyes and looked at me.

"It's done." He looked spent. The prayer truly did take the last of the good vibes out of him.

"Good, now put it on," I said. He complied as best he could, but he didn't understand what to do with the loop I had tied on one side of the bootlace. "May I?" I offered.

"Please," he said, as annoyed as a child fresh out of their Velcro shoes.

"First off." I set the necklace down and unbuttoned his first two buttons. "Your stifling collar is gone, so let's be rid of this as well. In fact..." I tugged at the top button, but my finger couldn't rip it free. "Let's just be rid of them altogether." I leaned over him and gnawed on the button with my teeth.

"Whoa." He shifted back slightly to let me get to it. His hands rose as if he thought he needed to be participating in the act somehow. "You are definitely not lacking confidence, are you?"

"I'm sure some part of me has some humility left," I mumbled over the task. "Just not with buttons." I spat out the choker button and moved on to the next one.

"Imagine what August would say if she walked in right now and saw you nibbling my buttons."

"Not half as much as she would if I was nibbling something else." I sat up and spat the other button across the room. Priest grinned ear to ear at me and I could feel myself start to blush at what I had just said.

"Speaking of your nibblers," I said, quickly slumping back away from him to look over the room and hide my face while it cooled. "Where is the harem?"

"Gone," he said simply. I looked back at him. He wasn't smiling anymore.

"Why?"

"You know why."

I frowned. "Are you going to bring them back?"

"I wouldn't know where they went." He shrugged.

I wiped my lips, feeling a little thread on them. "Are you going to start drinking again?" When he didn't answer I assumed he didn't have the answer, or didn't want to give it to me; either way I was reminded that he was an addict.

I wrapped the necklace around him and tied it to lie just above his sternum. I leaned back and touched the charm. It did look nice. I smiled at him and looked at my watch. I shrugged, offering him no explanation for needing to leave other than it being time.

"Thank you for this." He touched the necklace. "Thank you for my second chance as well."

"All in a day's work, or in this case, about a week. My hero training paid off." I headed to the door. There were moments with Priest when I knew I had overstayed my welcome, mainly when he started giving eyes to his women, or started jonesing for a hit. This wasn't one of them. This was the first time I felt truly welcome, and the fact that I had no desire to leave was just as new to me.

Too Many Issues, Not Drunk Enough To Deal With Them

"**S**PEAKING OF THE LAST three months..." Priest's voice rose enough to make the church sound hollow. "Would you like to talk about it?"

I turned back to face him. He was still sitting in his pew. I didn't bother giving him a fake smile. He knew the last three months weren't easy for me. A lot had happened; some good, some bad, and I was still deciding which was which. "Not really."

He nodded in understanding. "Would you like me to hold you? You could cry on my shoulder for as long as you like."

I chuckled, but it wasn't funny. It was the most honest offer of sympathy I could have ever hoped to receive. He wasn't insisting I sit through a session of psychoanalysis. He wasn't even suggesting I should cry or needed to cry, just that I could. It was permission to freely feel whatever I want to feel, without any purpose other than to feel it.

I didn't know how to respond to his offer. It was too simple to say "*yes*" or "*no*" to. The truth was, I didn't want to leave, and any excuse to stay might have appealed to me.

Priest raised his arm, inviting me back. I returned to the pew and sat beside him. I wasn't sure how to begin the process of being held.

He guided me into position, leaning me back across his lap, while I positioned my feet on the pew. He wrapped his arms around me and drew me against his chest. I draped over his shoulder like a baby needing to be burped.

It all felt strange and forced, but I let my head relax on his shoulder. He whispered a blessing that even at close proximity sounded like gibberish.

I started to enjoy the simplicity of the embrace. It wasn't tender like a "there, there, please stop crying so you don't snot on my shirt" hug. It was strong and pressing like an "I missed you so much, don't ever leave again" hug.

I could smell my floral shampoo on Priest's hair. It was by no means a manly scent, but clean was appealing no matter what the undertone.

I realized trying to cry wasn't going to work and I moved to push away, but he shifted his grip to press my head back to his shoulder. He wasn't going to let me go that easily.

I sighed and waited for him to tire of the experience, but he didn't seem to be in any rush. He was in essence hugging the pain out of me. It was an interesting and generous therapy. Unfortunately, it was also boring as hell.

That thought made me huff out a laugh. The vocalization of the opposing emotion spurred me into an unexpected hyperventilation. The last three months were suddenly on my doorstep and I knew I was about to lose it. Not just sad tears, but a complete and utter breakdown rarely seen in adulthood. This was not going to be pretty.

I tried to pull away again. This was too much, too fast; I needed space to get control. Priest didn't budge.

I panicked, feeling suffocated by my surfacing emotions. I couldn't get away from them, or from Priest. I was about to have an emotional climax. I could feel it coming, and I knew it would feel good to let it out, but I was so afraid of it, scared of all the anger and fear I had swallowed over the last three months, and my unforeseen disappointment at it all ending.

I squeezed Priest's back and ripped at his shirt, warning him I might explode if he let this continue. The tears were already rolling from my eyes, and my heaving breaths were so ragged that anyone listening would have been confused about the goal of my ascent.

Half in frustration, half in relief, I tumbled over the edge with a wail even the most sympathetic listener would have been uncomfortable with. I clawed at Priest's back, screaming irascibly against his stilled body.

I sucked up stuttered breaths like a child unable to reconcile the consequences of being an emotional being. At one point, I even bit Priest's shoulder, for no other reason than to punish him for letting me put myself through such an overload.

Through it all, he didn't move, he didn't speak; not to rub my back, and not to shush my wails. His stillness was impervious and consuming. I settled into a steady weep and let my body collapse against him. When I had no tears left to cry and every emotion had been drained dry—save one—I lifted my head and nuzzled his ear.

He relaxed his grip and I pulled myself to face him. There was only one other release I wanted and it had nothing to do with feeling bad. I touched his face and kissed his cheek, running increasingly frantic kisses toward his ear. I sucked his earlobe, and moved down his neck.

For a brief moment, I thought he might have orchestrated the whole thing to make me give in to desire with reckless abandon. I even questioned if this would officially tip the scales toward describing me as a slut.

Two different men only a week apart? Gasp!

Before I could get to the part where I denounced all propriety and forethought in lieu of pleasure, he said my name. Not *"Oh, Lenore keep going"* or *"Lenore, you vixen,"* but rather *"Lenore"* with the scolding question mark behind it.

"No," I whined, already knowing he was asking me to stop. I wanted to finish trailing kisses down his body, but the lack of enthusiasm on his part made me feel like I was playing checkers against myself, and I was cheating to win.

I huffed and pulled away without looking at him. He already knew my plot and grabbed my arms. "Lenore, look at me."

I repositioned to sit next to him instead of across him, and I stared at my feet. "I'm sorry." I sounded like a teenager who didn't want to apologize even though she knew she was in the wrong. "I got carried away with my emotions."

"I know. That's why I stopped you. Can you at least look at me, so I know you're not angry?"

"I thought you were angry," I said, looking up to him.

"Why, because a beautiful woman is kissing me?"

I wanted to respond with a coy dismissal, but it occurred to me that it would make it sound like I was fishing for more compliments. Besides that, what was Priest supposed to say? *"No, I don't want you; you're dog-ugly."* I could well have been dog-ugly and he still wouldn't say it.

"You should go home and get some rest. I know I've put you through hell the last few days."

"Yeah." I nodded, feeling a little bit more rejected. "Okay." I got up and headed to the door. I wasn't aware he was following me out until he caught the door over my head to hold it open.

"Lenore." I turned back, putting myself between the door and him. As inappropriate as my outburst of affection had been, I wondered if it was the beginning of a deep-end crush. "I'm going to need you to stay away from me for a while."

Or not.

I rolled my eyes and turned to walk out. The third little sting of rejection was starting to fester. He caught my arm, and I resisted the urge to twist out of it and pin it behind his back.

"I'm going to need a little alone time to make some decisions. You've brought a lot of things to my attention I had been ignoring, or was too doped up to understand. As much as I treasure having someone sober to talk to, I think those questions of sobriety you asked before need to be answered without the burden of disappointing you. The last thing you need is a lousy pot-smoking drunk making you promises he can't keep. And the last thing I need is another reason to hate myself. Do you understand?"

"Yeah," I murmured.

He chuckled and pinched my side, making me squirm. "Can you say that like you support me, and not like I kicked your puppy?"

I smiled, trying not to think about how much I would miss this calm, playful Priest when his sobriety went the way of the dodo. "Yes, I wholly support anything you wish to do to encourage your steps away from your crutches. Including you-know-who."

He smiled and leaned down to me. I hoped it was a kiss, since I still hadn't managed to give up on that notion yet. It *was* a kiss, but approximately six inches higher than I wanted it. My forehead rejoiced at the feel of his lips. I licked my lips in case he stopped there on the way by. He didn't.

"Lenore, go home." He nodded to the truck.

"For cripes' sake, I've tried to leave like three times already. Quit stopping me."

"Quit letting me." He smirked.

I opened my mouth to object, but he was already closing the door. Considering I was still leaning against it, I no longer felt the *sting* of rejection; I was immersed in the cold winter of it. Painful, but it was starting to numb me.

Speaking of cold, I was due for another shower.

Options

I T WAS PROBABLY A bad idea to knock on Devin's door right after I had gotten myself twitter-pated over a man that, up until recently, I hadn't even considered that good of a friend, but I was a glutton for punishment. More to the point, I was lonely.

I couldn't claim anything resembling love in regards to the men I'd fraternized with in the last week, but Garrett and Priest reminded me I was missing some necessary attentions. When Devin didn't answer, I determined he was probably spending the remainder of the evening in Haden's room. I felt a little twinge of guilt over that thought and headed back to my room.

Strangely enough, my room was the biggest one, but since my ceiling was so slanted, I didn't have much standing room. It worked for me since I always needed a place to pile my laundry without causing a traffic jam.

When I found Devin asleep on my bed with a full tub of popcorn and a bottle of soda, I smiled and shut the door quietly behind me. The remote control to my mini DVD player was clasped in his hand, and the blue screen on the television told me all he had to do was press play.

I slipped off my shoes and crawled in beside him.

"Hey," he said when he roused, wiping the sleep from his eyes.

"Movie night, huh?"

"Yeah." He leaned over and kissed me even before he could focus. "Where have you been?"

"Dropping off Priest," I said.

"That took a while," he pouted. "Did he behave?"

"Yes, he apologized for his aggression."

"They always do," he grumbled and resituated so I could rest against his shoulder. "Did you give him the necklace?"

"Yeah, he liked it. Or at least he pretended to."

"*I* liked it," Devin said flatly as if his opinion should be the only viable one. "Are you going back to see him soon?"

"No, supposedly he is going to try to get on the wagon, so he wants me to stay away."

"Do you believe him?" Devin frowned.

I grabbed some of the popcorn and put it on his chest so I could use him as an eating tray. His gray t-shirt was already full of grease from our previous movie nights. "No, but it sounds good in my head. I don't want to lose anyone else. It's a hard wish to fulfill, but I'll keep wishing for it."

"You know we all love you, right?"

"Yes." I smiled, thinking back to how they risked their lives to save me on the viaduct when I was in my bloodthirsty ego trance.

"You know I love you most of all, right?" He winked.

"Of course." I reached for some popcorn and he touched my hand.

"I love you like a little sister." He looked down at my hand and caressed the back of it. "But I can be more than that to you, if you need me to be."

He looked back at me and I smiled at him. He was a picture-perfect image of warmth and kindness. I couldn't imagine loving him more than I did at that moment. Given the state I was in, I should have thrown myself at him like a wild banshee in heat, but I didn't. His love alone quelled my desires and satisfied my needs.

"I know, and I love you even more for it." I leaned up and kissed him chastely on the lips. He didn't look disappointed that I didn't push for more, which was good, since his puppy-dog eyes might have broken my heart. "You were going to tell me about your tournaments."

His eyes brightened. "Yes, but let's watch the movie first." He squeezed me closer and I settled into his chest to watch the movie, nibble popcorn, and ruminate on the delight of having options.

The Tournaments

Since the watch rotation was already messed up, we decided to throw caution to the wind with a game of UNO poker. Haden, Devin, and I sat around the coffee table playing. August came in from her perimeter search and grabbed a beer from the fridge before getting comfortable on the couch behind us. I offered to deal her in, but she said she preferred to watch.

"Okay, tell me about the tournaments," I said, frowning at my cards. I was losing rather dramatically, but I didn't care. I tossed in a couple of red chips and quickly realized I had overplayed my hand. I reached to the ante to take one back and was promptly met with a slap from Haden. "Ouch!"

"No take-backs," she barked. She was, of course, winning because she was as aggressive at board games as she was in life.

"Geez, can you at least wait until I've got my ball gag in place, Madam Pagoda?" I muttered, rubbing my hand.

Haden and Devin exchanged a look.

"Who's Madam Pagoda?" Haden asked as she threw my coin back in my face.

I paused. "I have no idea." I laughed and they joined. "Sounds familiar, doesn't it?" I took a swig of my beer. It wasn't my first of the night, and it probably wouldn't be my last, but I was pacing myself in case I had to do something remotely heroic or speech-oriented. "So, tournaments!" I slapped the table. "I can't take the anticipation. What is it? Why are you so happy about it? And how interested should I pretend to be?"

"Pretend!" Devin pinched my toes under the coffee table. I tried not to squeal for Haden's sake, but I couldn't stifle my high-pitched yelp. For the most part, she had accepted my new friendlier relationship with Devin, especially since we still weren't having sex, but I didn't like to be too flirtatious in front of her. I wasn't sure she would see the difference in it the way Devin and I did.

"The Metro put together a monthly tournament for regular Joes such as myself," Devin started.

"Your name's not Joe," I pointed out with my dingy-blonde voice. He winked to let me know he was amused, but didn't stop talking.

"Anyone can compete for the top prize."

"Prize?" I perked my brow.

"Right now, it's just the namesake, but if I win the annual, I get a big plaque."

"Wow, back to the days when people were satisfied with trophies. How nostalgic. What do the competitions involve?"

"Every month is different. I did hand-to-hand combat. First, I fought one guy to get a base ranking. Next, I fought three grim to get my score and then I fought the guy I tied with and I won."

"You got a lucky hit," Haden mumbled.

"You're just sore because you didn't even make it past the first round."

"Those women were huge. I'm doing the sharp-shooting tournament next month. We'll see if I'm not competing with you in the finale after all." Haden tipped her brow at him. He gave her a wolfish grin that made me blush more than Haden.

"Once a month a different study then?" I asked, trying to break them up before I had to start fanning myself.

"Yes." Devin started counting them off on his fingers. "Freestyle hand-to-hand, martial arts, sharp-shooting, swordplay, strength, speed and endurance, creative warfare—that ought to be interesting—balance and agility, mental concentration, staff fighting, spear throwing, and *archery*."

Devin said the last part with a hint of excitement and finality. He raised his brow, expecting me to mirror his enthusiasm. I glared at him and looked back at August. She shrugged and shook her head.

"Don't look at me, this is all him," she said, reaching into my hand to play a card for me.

I laughed. "No," I said without any more thought than it might take me to consider going through the last three months again. Devin's face scrunched with shocked disappointment. I shook my head to reiterate my point before taking a swig of my beer.

"What? Oh, come on!" Devin whined. "I saw how fast you laid out those grim the other day. Your defensive skills aren't the only skills Garrett helped you improve."

A stray thought entered my mind and I choked on my beer. Sputtering over my misdirected beverage, I blushed with embarrassment. August patted my back in assistance.

"What?" I croaked.

"You could win that tournament, and what's more, all four of us could compete in the finale together. We can't lose."

I looked back at August. She tipped her head in a *why not* way.

"What are you competing in?" I asked, thinking she could compete in at least half of those categories.

"Swordplay." She smiled.

"Are you sure this isn't something you want me to do?"

August's smile faded. "Why don't you come with us to Haden's event in a few weeks? If it appeals to you, you can enter. If not, don't worry about it." I could see she was trying to offer me the option instead of forcing me to do it, but I could also see how important it was to her. I had already put myself through hell in the name of this woman. I wasn't sure I wanted to do anything more for her.

"I'll think about it," I said, giving her the only answer I could without disappointing her, or myself.

The Metro

The Metro. The Big O.

Once the mecca of state commerce, now... still the mecca, but with the added highlight of being a war zone for the fight against the grim. I hadn't seen it myself, but I was told a northern section of the city was fenced, barricaded, and heavily guarded to keep the grim consolidated and under control. Unlike the rest of the state that shot first and went for beer later, the people of the raging Metro took a more lawful approach to things.

On the eve of the city being taken over by the silver saints, the current and still acting mayor dedicated himself to creating a concentration camp to house the overwhelming infestation. Every crystalline dead—as such, inactive—was transported to the quarantined sector, where they were barricaded into buildings. The project only took days to achieve since everyone was more than willing to donate their time and energies to keep themselves safe.

The fully animated glimmer grim were hunted down by a task force made up of veteran military and police officers. In just under a month, the streets were cleaned up and the remaining population was safe to roam, as long as they stayed away from the northern part of the city, which was fine, since they were used to that anyway.

When the occasional break-out occurred, Jimmy the Card kept everyone up to date. He reported grim movements like his predecessors might have reported the weather or the traffic. As the break-outs increased in frequency and severity, the mayor chose to entertain different ways of getting rid of the grim without an all-out execution—which for some reason bothered people. Since it took me a good while to get used to killing them, I couldn't entirely blame them for their prudery.

That was where the tournament idea came from. It was a classic Caesarian misdirection. Hate your life? Hate the grim? Let's kill two birds with one stone. In this case, the competitors get to kill the grim, while the spectators get to enjoy a good show. Plus, there was bound to be hot dogs and beer.

Shot through the Heart...

DEVIN CRUSHED ME IN a bear hug after he lifted me out of the truck. We had arrived at the Qwest Center, the event center that was home to the tournaments. Judging by the number of cars crammed into the parking lot, it was a big deal.

The sun had just gone down and the cool night air was chilling me, but it was nothing compared to what it should have been in October.

"Thank you! Thank you! Thank you!" Devin squeezed me with his python grip. I usually appreciated his enthusiasm, but I could barely breathe, and I was pretty sure Haden might explode if she had to wait one more second to get checked in.

This month's tournament venue was firearms, and Haden was planning to compete. Or I should say, she was planning to win. I had tagged along to support and observe. I needed to determine if this was something I wanted to partake in myself.

"I haven't agreed to anything yet," I said, muffled by his shoulder.

"You will." He released me and pulled me along with his arm wrapped around me.

"Come on!" Haden growled.

Devin wrapped a firm arm around her as he walked by. I could tell she wanted to squirm away, but like me, she settled into the bathing attentions of our beautiful second sidekick. August waited for us to catch up. She smiled at our trio, linked by our pivotal man.

"Oh, August," Devin said as we caught up to her. "Why can't I have three arms?"

"I could always sit on your shoulders," she suggested, walking in stride a step ahead of us.

"That you could." He smirked. "I do enjoy having your thighs wrapped around my head."

Haden and I both smacked him. "TMI," Haden scolded him.

"Oh, ladies, you know there's enough of me to…" Even before he trailed off, Devin released us both and ran ahead to playfully wrestle and noogie some guy he recognized.

Haden and I slowed and looked at one another as if we had been simultaneously dumped for a better offer, which was kind of true.

"Well, that's just bully," Haden griped. "I'm going to go get checked in." She jogged ahead to the main entrance where a line was forming for the competitors.

The din of a second crowd drew my attention to the north. A quarter mile beyond the parking lot, I could see the border of the grim containment. The rotating lights, the pacing military men, and the circling helicopters, was just about as prison camp as it got. Even from several blocks away, I could see the grim pressed against the fence, reaching out to scratch, mar, or just plain rip the throats out of the passing guards.

"What are you thinking about?" August stepped up behind me. I had to resist the urge to lean back and rest my head on her shoulder.

"They're so close. Why do they even bother with them? They could bomb the whole section."

"It's not an easy decision for everyone," she said diplomatically.

"Do you suppose the rest of the world is debating the same thing? Desecrate the dead, or struggle with containment?"

"I think so. Some people can't let go. Some still believe they are saints. They believe the bodies should be bathed in holy water and buried in the earth."

"That's a lot of bodies to bury." I turned around to look at her. "What would you do? I mean, if it were feasible to keep them around. Would you bury them?"

She shook her head somberly and pressed on my back, gently urging me back into motion. I walked on with her, letting her decide the pace. "Do you know why we don't bury the crystalline dead?"

"Because digging sucks and they don't rot anyway, so why bother?"

August nodded. "Initially, we didn't know that though. We thought they were like any other bodies." I got the sense she was speaking for the entire human race when she said *we*. "After the apocalypse, we did bury some of them. Do you know what happened?" I shook my head. I loved story time with August. "The ground spat them back out," she said with slight merriment.

I laughed, but she didn't. "Wait, what do you mean? They..."

"A few weeks after we buried them, regardless of how deep, the bodies rose to the surface, expelled from the graves."

I shook my head, and she quirked an eyebrow, daring me to question her. I parted my lips to ask a thousand questions. Her eyes settled on something behind me, and she smiled. "Garrett, perhaps you can back me up on this?"

My eyes widened and I whipped around.

...and You're to Blame

GARRETT WAS NOT JUST behind me, but practically on top of me. He had crept up on me and I hadn't even noticed. More to the point, August hadn't even hinted at it. I couldn't help but step back into August. She rested her hand on my shoulder. She probably intended it to be consoling, but I took it wrong and pulled away from both of them.

Garrett was impassive, as usual. He appeared to be a little uncomfortable with our meeting, which was understandable since he left me the morning after I slept with him. I wasn't expecting to see him again, let alone this soon. Part of me was overjoyed—probably the part that wanted to sleep with him again—and another part of me was on guard prepared for his attack—probably the part of me that still bore the scars of his *training*.

"Garrett," I managed to say. My gaze jumped between him and August. I didn't want to reveal anything, but I was concerned I was revealing everything. The strange thing was, I didn't even know anymore what I was hiding. Did August already know? Had she seen the scars? Did she suspect I had slept with her brother? Was she okay with that?

"I see you've let all my progress go to shit," Garrett scolded August, while managing to offer me a healthy share of his glare.

"I had her preoccupied. Besides, no one ever hears you coming, you serpentine bastard."

Garrett leaned in and gave his sister a kiss on the cheek. He glanced at me and I gave him a small smile. Not so big that he thought me desperate and not so small that he thought I was still mad at him. I should have been mad, but I was so happy to see him again.

"Are you competing?" Garrett asked. He turned back to his sister without giving our intimate connection the slightest acknowledgment. I felt like a third wheel in the conversation. Maybe even a spare tire.

"No, Haden is."

Garrett scoffed. "You could win this easily," he said. I looked to August to see if this were true. She averted her eyes. "You and your damned sword."

"I like my sword," she defended. "It doesn't run out of ammunition."

"But it can run out of power," he said, squeezing her ample biceps.

"Same old argument." She shook her head. "I take it you're competing."

He scratched his head. "Yeah, I think I might have a shot, no pun intended."

I chuffed at the obscure yet lame joke. No one joined me and Garrett all but rolled his eyes at me. I furrowed my brow at him, baffled that he could be this offish to me after seeing me naked. Wasn't that supposed to make men like you?

"How is she doing?" he asked, looking me over as if I was a car he had recently sold her. The ache in my chest was more than pain; it was outrage. I couldn't bear this.

"Lenore," August pronounced carefully in case her brother had forgotten my name, which seemed entirely possible at that point, "is doing fine." Garrett tipped his head. "She can run now, and her archery skills—"

"Did you even test her?" His voice pitched with condescension.

"Yes, but… She has not responded to my tests well." August looked sympathetically at me, as if she didn't want to be a tattle-tale, but had no choice. "She won't defend herself against me."

Garrett shook his head. "You're telling me she let you hit her?" His reproachful look told me I was in trouble if this were true.

"Well, I didn't actually hit her, I just…"

"August! I spent three months training her so you didn't have to do the hard labor. *Of course* she won't defend herself. She knows you'll never actually hit her!"

"I'm not going to bludgeon her just to see if she learned anything."

"How do you think I trained her?" August's eyes widened as she tried to rationalize what he was saying. She opened her mouth to speak on the point, but she couldn't address the issue while she was still comprehending it. "I'll show you what she can do." Garrett stalked to me and raised his fist to punch me.

Stubborn

I T HAD BEEN DECIDED somewhere along the line that I was, in fact, not lazy, but really, really stubborn. I'm not entirely sure there was a difference between the two, but it did invoke a better image.

When Garrett came at me, I instinctively tensed, set my feet, and shifted my right shoulder forward. If I only wanted to get away, I had the option to duck and backpedal. Those were early lessons, though. Garrett had taught me in the later lessons to block his punch and take the opening for all its worth.

The danger with that option was his sixty-pound advantage, and his meaty fists were likely only going to be slowed by my block. That's why the uppercut to the chin is best. The nerve running along the chin is like a shut-off switch to the brain. Pain for me; knockout for him.

When he came at me, I had already positioned myself to fight back. However, between the sour looks he was giving me, and the brusque way he addressed me, I decided not to give him the satisfaction. Neither he nor August were going to play puppet with my strings. Punch or no, at least it was my choice, not theirs. I released my fists, and relaxed my neck for the incoming head volley.

His fist hit hard, as I knew it would. The gasp I heard from August was priceless. I absorbed the impact as much as I could, while keeping my feet planted. I blinked away the stars and turned to face Garrett's irritated shock. His anger reared and he punched me in the stomach to force some kind of a defense from me. I was no doubt embarrassing him. All I could do was tense and hope I was making my point once and for all. Whatever that point was, I had already forgotten.

"Garrett, stop!" August shouted.

Garrett looked down at me, settling on my eyes. He must have recognized the look on my face. It was the same look I gave him right before I smashed his face in. "You stubborn little b—"

His insult was cut off by a tackle from the side.

Say it Ain't So

IT WAS TRUE AUGUST was always my hero. No matter where I was, what I was doing, if I was in danger, she was magically there. I don't mean to say she had super powers—although that could still be debated—but she was a very good hero.

In most situations nothing would have changed that, but over the last few weeks, Devin had become my number one fan. He was like a brother, a lover—minus the sex—and a loyal puppy all rolled into one. I presumed some of the extra attention was out of guilt for leaving me behind, but also, I think he missed me.

It was a toss-up of which one was going to come to my rescue. When it turned out to be neither of them, I was a little disappointed, yet pleasantly surprised.

It didn't take Haden long to wrestle Garrett down and stick her Glock nearly up his nose. "Don't you fucking move!" she shouted at him.

"What's going on?" Devin's run came to a halt beside August. He looked over the scene. Haden on top of Garrett, August stunned beyond words, and me, doubled over with a bloody nose.

"This asshole hit Lenore!" Haden yelled, jerking Garrett's collar. He lay on the ground beneath her, quiet and defenseless. His gun was out of reach on his waistband under Haden's knee—as she intended it to be.

Devin came to me, but I waved him off. I didn't want to be touched, let alone consoled in front of Garrett. Must be strong in front of the man who beats you. What's the difference between bravery and pride again?

"Lenore! Why didn't you stop him?" August admonished me. "I saw you shift. You were ready for him. You stopped at the last second. Why?"

"Because she's stubborn!" Garrett yelled. Haden shifted her gun to cold-cock him and I shook my head in disapproval. She opened herself up. Her first mistake was not tossing his gun right away. Her second mistake was staying on top of him. Her third mistake was moving her barrel away from the target.

Garrett grabbed her hands and flipped her over his head with the help of his strong legs. Before she could recover, he was up and pointing his gun back at her. "Looks like I could teach you a thing or two as well," he vaunted.

"Garrett!" August scolded him and he immediately put away his gun. "Haden!" It took a little longer for Haden, but eventually she holstered hers.

"What the hell is going on?" Devin asked again, not satisfied with the aftermath display.

"I won't dance for them, and he's pouting... with his fists," I answered.

Garrett approached me and Devin stepped in his way. "You don't touch her again," Devin snarled.

"Garrett, we didn't need to test her here," August objected. "Why did you hit her so hard? I think you broke her nose."

"What?" I instinctively reached for my nose. It felt swollen. "Oh man! I don't want a bent nose!" Everyone glanced at me like they couldn't believe that was the only thing I was worried about.

"It's not that bad," Garrett said, eyeing me from behind the wall of Devin. "If you call off your playboy here, I'll check it."

"I'll take care of it," August volunteered and came over to look at me. She raised her hand to touch me and I batted her away. "Lenore..."

"Why are you coddling me now? The damage is done."

"I didn't know he was going to punch you. I thought he was just going to scare you."

I laughed hard and loud. The only one who got the joke was Garrett, but he didn't join in. Everyone else looked concerned by my maniacal reaction, which made the resentment I was harboring that much stronger.

"I don't mean *now*. I mean, why are you coddling me after my training is over? Your sympathy for my pain is useless. Your heroics against my abuser are too little, too late. You wanted me trained. I'm trained. You just didn't ask him how he was going to do it!"

"Garrett?" August looked to her brother with the question Devin never wanted to ask me. "I told you to go slow with her."

"We did go slow." Garrett moved around Devin to stand behind me. He was in view of everyone but me. I tensed as instinct taught me, or perhaps that was one of Garrett's lessens as well. "Didn't we, Lenore?" I didn't nod, but I tilted my head to keep him in my peripheral vision. "Once we established we weren't playing anymore, we made great strides."

Everyone looked at me for the answer and I shook my head. "You wanted me trained," I said flatly turning all their ire for Garrett back on them. "I'm trained. Every scar was a lesson learned from a mistake not to be repeated." I pulled my hair aside to show the full length of my head scar that went through to the bone. Devin grimaced at the view. Haden looked like she was seeing it for the first time. August just looked down. She must have suspected it was a hard three months, but she didn't realize *how* hard.

"So, thank you for defending me, but Garrett's fists are the least of my concern. I imagine this—" I touched my cheek under my eye where the majority of the pain was, "—is the only way he knows how to say hello to me."

I looked back at him. The expression on his face was a little dumbfounded, but not enough for me to feel I'd succeeded in anything. "*Hi,* by the way." I walked off, not offering anyone the opportunity to say anything to make me feel better, or make themselves feel better.

Dirty Laundry and Dirtier Bathroom Stalls

IT'S FUNNY HOW PEOPLE will ignore you if they think you are emotionally troubled, but the minute they see your face is beat to hell, they start to worry. The assumption must be that if someone is truly troubled they would reach out and ask for help, but they never do. That was perhaps why I appreciated Priest's offer so much. He knew I didn't want to talk, and probably didn't need to talk, but I did need to cry, even if I didn't want to.

I got a few looks on the way to the restroom, but in this type of place, it probably wasn't unusual to see a few black eyes. As it was, nearly everyone I passed had a gun in their hand or holster. I wondered if I shouldn't have asked Haden to come with me, since she was my new hero.

I entered the long galley bathroom and did a double take at two women making out against the wall between the air dryers. At least someone was having fun. I bent myself over the sink basin and washed the blood from my nose and lip. It was starting to hurt more and the bruising under my eye was already dark red.

I laughed at my mirror image. I thought I was done with bruises. The two lesbians joined me by the mirror and handed me a paper towel and a freshly lit homemade cigarette. I took both. I blotted my face off and noted their kindness might have been them hitting on me. I was never sure what the rules of the new world were. Were threesomes back in, or had they never gone out?

"Poor baby, did your man do d'at to you?" The woman on my left was black and covered in shiny diamonds. With a little less bling she might have looked elegant. Her New Orleans accent was a refreshing change to the mumbled drawl I was used to.

"Something like that," I said. Her friend, as white as white could be, with a shaved head and as many piercings as New Orleans had diamonds, clicked her tongue and tipped her head in sympathy to that.

"You best give up on d'em men." New Orleans leaned over the counter to look at me in the mirror. "D'ey nothing but trouble. We can give you anything d'at man can, and twice as good, and twice as long."

"Mm-hmm," Buzz Cut agreed.

I smiled even though I was uncomfortable as hell. I took a drag of the cigarette and all at once I realized it was pot. I hadn't smoked tobacco more than twice in my life, so marijuana was even more trying to my lungs. As I coughed, the girls took it upon themselves to pat my back.

"Sorry, I thought that was a cigarette." I handed the joint back to them.

"D'at's okay, why don't you give it another try?"

"Pot is the new cigarette," Buzz Cut added when I didn't take the joint.

I was well aware I was being hit on at this point, but I decided being punched in the face might warrant a little drug experimentation. I shrugged and took the joint. Before I could take the hit, Garrett yelled at me from the door.

"Lenore, no!" He marched over, scattering the girls. He ripped the joint out of my hands and crushed it on the floor under his foot. He turned to the irritated women and shooed them like they were crows. "Get out!"

They glared back at him, but shuffled out the door. I stared after them, confused. "Crap, Garrett, since when are you so anti-drug?"

"Did you take a drag?" he asked, looking me over for signs of it.

"No—well I did, but I couldn't hold it."

"Shit." He rubbed his chin stubble. "Do you feel okay?"

"I don't think pot hits you that fast."

"I'm not worried about the pot. I'm worried about what they spiked it with." I looked down at the crushed joint, futilely trying to see what he was referring to. "Those were gang *scangers*!" he shouted as if I should know what that meant. He rolled his eyes. "Boy, you *are* a country mouse. They drug women and take them home to rape and molest like live blow-up dolls. Some of them will pimp women out on the street to whoever is willing to offer good drugs for a nearly passed-out woman."

My eyes must have come out of my head, because he put his hand out to stop me from fleeing the bathroom and the whole damned city. "It's okay though," he said softly. "They won't come back."

I hugged myself. Crap, what a bad night. "What do they spike the pot with?"

"Roofies, Ecstasy, something to make you... pliable."

I groaned and turned back to the sink and splashed cold water on my face. When I looked up he was watching me through the mirror. "What are you doing here?"

"I came to check on you. Straighten your nose if necessary."

"I don't mean that." I turned and he moved in to check my nose. I instinctively tensed at his proximity, but I was more than familiar with his Mr. Fix-It side. He yanked on my nose, and I winced at the pain. "I mean here in the O. I thought you went back to Chicago."

"I did. I came back for the tournament."

I hadn't expected him to come back just for me, but he still hadn't acknowledged the relationship we had developed over three months of close proximity. Which was insulting to my ego... and my heart.

"Well, have fun with that." I turned back to the sink to fluff my hair. "I won't be cheering for you, but don't assume it's because of Haden."

"Don't be mad at me because you wouldn't defend yourself," he scolded. "August was right. You were ready for me and you gave up."

"I didn't give up, you arrogant ass! I stood up!" I yelled at him through the mirror. "I am not going to be your fucking puppet! Anyway, I'm not mad because you hit me! I've gotten used to that by now."

"Why are you mad then?" he asked, throwing his arms up. I crossed my arms and turned around to face him. My eyes double-dog dared him to guess why. He flushed. "Look, Lenore, I told you I couldn't stay with you."

"That's not... We can come back to the subject of a fling versus a one-night stand, because there is a difference. What I'm mad about is you didn't even say hello to me, you asshole."

"I wasn't sure how to handle you, given how much I'd put you through, including the one-night stand."

"Well, you start out with a greeting; pick your favorite. Then you ask *me* how I've been, instead of talking to your sister about me like I'm a lab rat."

"I didn't want to... August doesn't need to know about us... I mean, what I do is my business."

"Oh, my god, you're such a dick!" I stomped toward the exit.

"Hello, Lenore." Garrett said it without ire, and perhaps even smoothly, if that was possible with only two words. It stopped me in my tracks. "You look well. Aside from where some dirtbag decided to overstep his boundaries." I turned back with a slight smirk. He was smooth when he wanted to be. Too bad he didn't want to be very often.

"You look good too. It's good to see you." It was good to see him. I may not have missed the endless training, but I had missed him.

Did Someone Say Ecstasy?

IT WAS PROBABLY THE drugs. I had only had a little bit, but there was no other explanation for me diving on Garrett like he was a fresh batch of cookies. He was momentarily shocked and tensed for battle, but as soon as my tongue forced its way into his mouth, he came around.

He grabbed at me, pulling my body against his. When he moved his hands to my arms in an attempt to get control of the situation, I pulled his pelvis against my hip. He pulled away with a groan and took a few breaths. Perhaps he wasn't pulling away, so much as searching for air.

"Lenore, I still can't be with you."

"I know," I said, kissing and licking down his neck until a reached his t-shirt. Clothes suck.

"I'm leaving after the tournament. I won't see you. This is all we would have."

"Why are you still wearing your pants?" I ground out while I reached into his pants for the real feel. He wrenched away despite the moan of pleasure escaping his lips. This was almost certainly the drugs.

"Okay, okay, slow down, though. Save some for yourself." He tried to push me to the counter, but I pushed him into one of the stalls.

We immediately left that stall and found another. I wanted sex, not dysentery.

After a quick discussion, it was decided that his pants would stay on, slightly lowered, with the fly open. I on the other hand disrobed the lower half, and used the front clasp on my bra for the purpose it was intended.

With my t-shirt behind my neck and my panties around my wrist lest they touch anything in the bathroom, I took my place on my throne. I nearly climaxed from the pleasure of his insertion. That was definitely the drugs.

Never Enough Time or Apologies

"LET'S GO AGAIN," I said even though I knew I had spent him.

"I can't. I'm going to be late for the preliminaries."

"Oh crap, I still have to watch this damn tournament," I whined, but quickly retrieved some hope for a happy ending. "We should hook up after, before you leave, okay?"

"I'll try," he said.

"That means no." I rolled my eyes.

He pulled me down for a hard kiss. "I'll try, but I can't exactly pull you into a bathroom after the tournament. There won't be an empty stall for miles." I nodded, disappointed, even though I knew by the time the tournament was over I would probably be regretting this rendezvous as it was. "Is this one of mine?" he asked, touching one of my now many scars. He tickled my stomach and I flinched. The giggle I couldn't help but let out made him smile. That was a rare treat.

"That's my appendix scar."

"I thought so. I know what my handiwork looks like." He lost his smile, though I wasn't sure why, since he was the one trying to make light of the scars.

"Well, you stitched most of them up, you should recognize them," I said to assure him I wasn't holding him entirely accountable for doing August's dirty work.

He touched one such scar marring my belly. It was from a broken beer bottle. Not so much from him, but from my inability to control my weapon during a fight. "That one made me want to stop." He looked up at my head and pushed my hair back to see the long gouge from the fire ax. "That one too."

"They all kind of made me want to stop." I was intending it as a joke, but he grimaced.

"You know I can't apologize for any of these, don't you?"

"Why, because you'll lose the advantage of me being afraid of you?"

"Are you... afraid of me?" His face looked pained. I knew he would have been wounded if I said "*yes*."

"You've hurt me a lot, but you've given me a good deal of pleasure too." I flexed my groin for effect, since I hadn't dismounted yet. "I'm not afraid of you in this position."

He rubbed my arms, which made me break out in goosebumps. "I can't apologize for them, because I'm proud of them. I'm proud of what I've forced you to become." I nodded. I wasn't sure how to respond to that. "Also... you're going to hate me for this, but I think they're kind of hot." I scrunched up my nose at the idea of him preferring my body with scars.

Before I could reply, he pulled my face down for a kiss. He pulled on my shoulders, driving me onto him. I hadn't even realized he had revived. I responded in kind, widening my stance to better receive his generous second helping.

The Mecca of Mecca

B Y THE TIME I met back up with August and Devin in the main entryway, they looked wrought with concern. I could sense they wanted to comfort me, and explain, and—blah, blah, blah. I was running on a high from good sex and the energetic cheering vibrating through the stadium like heavy bass. I didn't want to talk about my past. I was actually getting excited to see the tournament.

"Oh, don't be such sourpusses," I said coming up. "I'm fine."

Devin approached me prepared to take me in his arms, but at the last second he flinched, concerned he might break me. I wrapped my arm around his waist instead, and he kissed the top of my head. August looked at ease to see me calm, but worry was still etched on her face.

"Did my brother find you? He wanted to check on you, even though I insisted he leave you alone."

"Yeah, he found me. He sorted out my nose. We both yelled and screamed for a bit, but I think we're satisfied now." I almost smiled at my inside joke, so I changed the subject. "Where's Haden?"

"She's inside," Devin said. "The preliminaries have already started. You still want to watch, don't you?"

I could have told him I wanted ice cream and he would have driven me straight to a walk-in freezer at a DQ, but I knew how much he wanted to see the games. Plus, it would be super rude to not support my new savior.

"Of course I want to see the tournament. It sounds like a concert in there." I nodded in the general direction of the hoopla.

"Oh, you're going to love this, Lenore." He took my hand and led me. August strolled behind us with a slight smile, amused by Devin's boyish excitement as well. "This place is packed with people, some of them from three states away. Apparently we aren't the only ones starved for some excitement."

Devin released my hand to open the door for me. A wave of noise and heat hit me. It was enough to make me pause, but the awe of it drew me in. I had been in stadiums before, I had been to concerts, and football games, but there was something different about the atmosphere of this occasion.

Perhaps it was because I hadn't been in the presence of more than a dozen live humans in over a year. Or perhaps it was the electrical energy that people naturally produce when they are joined together in one common goal. I thought it was something else, though. This event was a reincarnation of an entertainment not permitted publicly in centuries. The crowd wasn't shaking the stadium floor because they wanted a high score. They wanted blood.

I felt the energy sink in as I got a view of the first stage of the tournaments, which had already begun. The first ranking would rule out the least skilled marksmen. The arena was filled with sand, amplifying the Roman coliseum imagery. The competitors stood in line like old west gunfighters ready for a showdown. Grim lined the other side of the arena, caged like horses before a run, their clothes distinctive to their lane.

The horn sounded and the grim were released. Unlike horses, the grim jumped out with no agenda other than killing. Some ran straight at their shooters. Others ran sideways in an attempt to get to the *handlers*. The shooters fired at their specific grim regardless of how off track they got.

The guns fired. Most of the grim went down with one shot, some took two. The few stragglers that were missed twice by their shooters were given bullets in the head by sharp-shooters in the rafters. I looked up at the military personnel dangling in crow's cages 30...40... a bunch of feet up. The mayor had outdone himself to ensure the safety of the competitors, as well as the crowd.

Devin guided me along by the elbow, since I was no longer looking where I was going. I was vaguely aware of the goofy smile I had on my face. Once we arrived at our high balcony seats, Devin pulled on my arm and patted my butt to sit. I did so without any question or concern that he would lead me wrong.

He leaned over to my ear and spoke loudly. "Magnificent, isn't it?" My smile widened and I grabbed his hand to squeeze it. He squeezed back. I was aware he was watching me more than the games, but I was too stricken to care.

Around the bend from us was a series of box seats normally reserved for VIPs. I could see our illustrious mayor and his entourage. They were golf-clapping for the festivities and drinking wine—anything to distinguish themselves as better than the surrounding honky-tonk beer drinkers.

One of his minions caught my eye. He was attractive—not the model that our own Devin was, but certainly a diamond in the rough of fat, old, graying politicians. He was a blond Ken doll, with perfect natural waves that looked like he spent hours gelling into position. His charcoal suit jacket and cream turtleneck sweater screamed rich, but informal.

Since no one and everyone was rich now, the status no longer mattered, but you could still tell who came from money and who didn't—usually by the number of double negatives they used. The most appealing thing about the intriguing stranger was his relaxed I'm-just-watching-the-game-with-my-friends-leg-up-on-the-rail pose.

His head turned to scan the crowd, and I could see the determination in his face. He was searching for something or someone. I smiled, wishing I could be that someone. I was definitely high. I'm such a lightweight.

His search ended... on me. Amused by the fortuitous connection, I giggled and covered my mouth. I looked behind me to see if I was misinterpreting his perspective. When I turned back he pointed at me, indicating, *"yes, you."* I yelped and sunk in my chair shyly.

"What are you doing?" Devin asked, leaning over to me.

"I think I'm flirting." I busted out with laughter. Yes, definitely high.

Devin scanned the crowd, but my blond Ken had looked away from me. Damn.

"What is wrong with you?" he asked. I could see August's disapproving look on my right. I turned to speak so only Devin could hear me.

"I think I'm high," I whispered.

His face displayed concern, amusement, confusion, and even a little anger, before he settled on amused disapproval and wrapped his arm around me. I glanced back at my admirer. As if on cue, he turned to me and blew me a kiss. I beamed and buried my head in Devin's shoulder.

What the hell was I doing?

Hip Hip Hurray!

MY POT BUZZ LEFT as quickly as it came, but the roar of the crowd and Devin's untamable enthusiasm kept me going long after. A beer in one hand and a hot dog in the other, I cheered and jeered with the rest of them. I was never much of a sports fan, but live theater yes, and this was *life or death* theater.

When Haden stepped up for the scoring challenge, I couldn't help but scoot to the edge of my seat. I wanted to press my palms together to pray for a good outcome, but even as my arms started to raise, August took my hand in hers, squeezing it hard. It was still two hands pressed together, just two different ones. I couldn't help but smile when I saw she had the same antsy expression on her face.

Haden cracked her neck and stared down the arena at the paneled corral stalls that held grim instead of cattle. As I understood it, her gun held fifteen shots. She had used up one on the first round with a dead-on shot to the head, which meant she had fourteen left to shoot at the ten grim about to be released. If she missed on any shot she would have a disadvantage in the final round.

The faster she shot, the better the score; the more accurate the shot—head, heart—the better the score. Misses were deductions, as were leg and arm shots, since they weren't usually enough to stop a grim. Not to mention the sharp-shooters weren't taking protective shots until her entire clip was empty.

The horn blew and I watched Haden concentrate on her first five distance shots. She ignored the three fast runners that were barreling right at her and took out the slow ones. I gripped August's hand hard.

"Why is she doing that? She needs to get the fast ones," I said, nearly lifting off my seat to yell at her.

"She knows what she's doing," August said confidently even though she was clutching my hand just as hard.

Haden took down two more that were veering off to find closer prey. A nervous handler waved happily after she shot an approaching grim. I was practically kneeling, I was so far off my chair. If she didn't shoot her forward attackers soon, I was going to tip over the railing. I couldn't even think beyond *please*.

The remaining three angled into her from their previous starting points. They were about to pounce on her in quick succession. At the last nail-biting second, she sidestepped and shot the first one.

Her shift in position brought the approaching grim from an angled sequential attack to a straight line with her aim. The first grim's head shattered like glass. The second shattered almost simultaneously. By the third, the bullet had slowed, but his face cracked and fell to the ground, the bullet costing him a good quarter of his noggin on impact. Haden had killed three birds with one stone.

It took a millisecond for the crowd to realize what she had done and we all erupted. I screamed louder than I thought possible, jumping up with August's hand still in mine. When I realized I had nearly yanked her arm off, I let her go and hugged her. I turned back to Devin and he scooped me up and twirled me, wooing all the way.

He gave me a wet kiss I knew he intended for Haden, but since I was the only one there, he made do. When he put me back down, we both screamed our hearts out at Haden and waved frantically to get her attention.

When Haden looked up us, she gave us a reserved nod, but I knew she was holding her smile at bay. She no doubt wanted to celebrate as much as we were, but since she hadn't officially won yet, it would have been tactless to do so. Devin blew her kisses, and I did the same, even though she rolled her eyes at me.

I wiped away the joyful tears that were creeping down my cheeks. August noticed and put her arm around me. "What's wrong?" She furrowed her brow.

I shook my head and shrugged. "I'm just so happy."

"You're proud of her," she said more than asked.

"That's so stupid, I know."

"Why is that stupid?" August asked, tugging on my shoulder.

"She's the second sidekick. Me being proud of her is like a student being proud of her teacher."

"Pride bestowed on others is just a compliment to the action and a measure of their love for the recipient." I looked up at her. "It has nothing to do with rank." I was about to respond with a joke to lighten the sensei talk, but I was rendered mute by the sudden presence of my Ken doll standing behind August.

"Excuse me," his voice thrummed like a bass guitar. "Is she with you?" He pointed to Haden.

August pulled me back toward my seat before releasing me. She turned to face the man, pointedly putting herself between us. "Who's asking?"

Ken looked chagrined, but he smiled warmly despite the insult of her immediate distrust. "My apologies. My name is Adrian Dorn." He reached out his hand to shake August's but she crossed her arms. I was surprised she was being so rude. I peeked over her shoulder and Adrian smiled at me. "Hello."

"I'm Lenore, this is August." I threw my hand out beside August to shake his still-outstretched hand, but August slapped it away and Devin pulled me back. I glared at him, but he gave me a stern look that told me I needed to let August handle this.

"Good to meet you, Lenore, August." Adrian bowed as if we were in the middle of a Jane Austin book. "I am the director of the games. I merely wanted to congratulate you on your friend's success. I've never seen anything like it."

"She loves guns," I said without thinking. Devin squeezed my elbow and pulled me against him—a not-so-understated request for me to be quiet. He wrapped his arm across my chest like a shield. His overprotective side was turning territorial. It seemed unnecessary, but then again, I had already been punched, drugged, and almost raped by lesbian scangers, so... I really needed to shut up.

"I can see that," Adrian said with a smile.

"Is there something more you wish to convey, Mr. Dorn?" August said with well-disguised contempt. "I find it hard to believe you came all this way to congratulate her victory."

"It was hardly a hike, my dear." Adrian revealed a little of his annoyance, but quickly corrected his tone. "However, I did want to offer you better seats for the final round. Your friend is no doubt unbeatable at this point, but you would have a better view for her final presentation in one of our box seats."

"We see rather well from here," August said flatly.

"Please, I must insist. The mayor himself requested I make the offer. If he sees you haven't taken the seats, it would be insulting to his offer."

August glanced over at the box seats where the mayor was sitting. I could see him nod and applaud us like we should be honored to be associated with Haden. August sighed. She couldn't in good conscience turn down such a compliment from the mayor. Some social niceties still needed to remain intact.

"Where are the seats?"

"I'll escort you."

He led the way to our box seats which were spitting distance to the contestants and their targets. Haden was still making rounds, and eyed our sudden change of view and the man escorting us to it.

Why was everyone so suspicious?

Adrian stopped at the start of the front row in the box and offered August leave to take the first seat. She glanced back at Devin as she did. There was apparently some secret sidekick language I had yet to be taught. Devin placed a hand on my shoulder as I came by Adrian. It wasn't so much like he was claiming me as property, but like he had every intention of pulling me back if Adrian suddenly exploded.

"Lenore," Adrian drawled as I passed by. I tried not to smile, but he was so 1980s soap opera star cute. "Am I mistaken, or were you the one I caught ogling me earlier?"

I chuckled, glancing at August. She was shaking her head ever so slightly to whatever silent question Devin had asked her. "I'm not sure women ogle so much as window shop, but yes, that was me. I'm sorry for the spectacle. I'm a little out of sorts. Tonight, has proved to be a rollercoaster of emotions."

"I can see that." He nodded, pointing to his own eye to refer back to mine, which by now would be an unhealthy blue. "Everything all right?" He glanced surreptitiously at August like he was accusing her of being my abuser. Perhaps in a roundabout way that was true, but I found the suggestion of needing protection from my own heroine impertinent.

"No, I'm fine." I looked to August, who was still watching our conversation like it was a test of my loyalty. "Thank you for the seats."

"It was the mayor's request. I'm just the errand boy," he said humbly.

"Well, convey our gratitude. We didn't mean to insult you. We just aren't used to openhandedness in the new world."

"Isn't that the truth?" He raised his brow. "Well, I'll leave you to it. It was nice meeting you." He held up his hand to shake. I got the feeling I shouldn't have taken it, but it was automatic.

He smiled warmly as he gripped my hand. It should have been fireworks and electrical attraction, but it wasn't. It was the exact opposite—repellent. The desire to be free of his hand was foreign and only comparable to the desire to keep your feet off the floor at night so the monster under your bed doesn't get you.

I smiled back at him, trying to hide my discomfort, as any polite person might. He lifted my hand to kiss it. I couldn't bear that. I was already trying to crawl out of my own skin. At the last second, I ripped my hand away. The feeling of a depraved ax murderer chasing me left immediately.

"I'm so sorry," I sputtered. Adrian's eyes cooled to my indiscretion. I might as well have thrown a drink in his face. "My hands are filthy. Have you seen the bathrooms in this place?" I grimaced, playing the fool to my own charade. "I couldn't possibly put your lips through that." I looked over his lips as if they were still appetizing to me. I tucked my own lips in, and looked away, feigning embarrassment for my thoughts. "Thank you," I said, clearing my throat and ducking into my seat.

"You're very welcome," he said after I sat and looked back at him. Devin and Adrian exchanged looks, sizing each other up. Neither seemed to like what they saw, but when no immediate risk was detected, Devin sat and Adrian walked away.

Even with the silent communication between August and Devin behind my back, I managed to ignore them and pretend to enjoy myself. All the while, my mind was straying back to remnants of the creepy crawlies that Adrian had left with me.

And the winner is...

THE COMPETITION FOR SECOND place in the final round was tough. Haden had already earned first place since there was no chance of beating her. Garrett was among the second-place competitors, and despite what I told him, I did cheer for him. I was secretly hoping he would look over and smile at me, but that wasn't so much a fantasy as a delusion.

Devin and August seemed a little baffled that I would cheer for him after what happened, but they didn't understand. Been there, done that. If I had forgiven him for the first fifty punches, there was no point in holding a grudge against one more. It was the mantra of the battered wife, but it applied here as well. If they were surprised by my cheers, they would have had heart attacks if they knew I had sex with him on a toilet a few hours ago.

However, in hindsight, that did sound a little shameful. And gross.

The three competitors tied for second place were blindfolded and spun for their competitive round of *pin the bullet on the grim*. They were then released one by one in the center of the arena where four grim were fast approaching. They were to use their remaining ammo to shoot the grim—easier said than done in light of the dizzy spell.

The first man didn't have enough bullets, and he had to use the butt of his gun to kill his fourth grim. It wasn't worth as many points since he should have conserved his ammunition, but the crowd loved it.

The second man was so dizzy he shot one of the handlers. Without question, he was immediately disqualified. Shooting innocent people was apparently frowned upon. Given the efforts the mayor had taken to ensure safety, that was no surprise.

Haden didn't seem to take any time to recover from her dizzy spell. Her shots were accurate and quick. Compared to her second round, it was almost boring, but still a triumph.

Garrett was the last up, and he had plenty of bullets. Assuming he didn't miss, he would win second place. I wasn't on the edge of my seat, but I did find myself wiggling my foot a little too enthusiastically. August looked at me, trying to discern my thoughts. I leaned over to her, keeping my eyes on the arena. "Is it wrong to hope he misses?"

"I don't imagine that it is, from your perspective."

I chuckled and sat back in my seat to feign a yawn. When all four of Garrett's bullets hit dead-on in the heads of the grim, I cheered and clapped. I shrugged at August, pretending I was a little disappointed he hadn't lost.

Haden and Garrett took their places alongside the third-place winner—the guy who didn't shoot a civilian. The master of ceremonies, AKA Jimmy the Card himself—who was apparently broadcasting live from the event—announced them as champions. I couldn't help but laugh at the radio personality. He was a scrawny freckled redhead with no business operating the voice box he had.

Garrett seemed a little perturbed at taking second place, but he could hardly argue with how cool Haden's shot was. Either way, he would be in the grand finale in ten months, so there was no reason to be pouty, except for his wounded pride. That was one area I had very little sympathy for.

Failure to Meet Potential

A FTER THE ANNOUNCEMENTS, HADEN was held back for photos and political mumbo jumbo—the type of stuff I had hoped would disappear after the reckoning. Apparently there were too many politicians left behind for it to disappear for good.

By the time we got out of the event center, the parking lots were nearly empty. No one liked hanging around this close to the northern camp after dark. I couldn't say I blamed them. Even with the military on high alert and the tall, uselessly electrified fences, the grim still looked ominous.

As we reached our lot, I heard the sound of a familiar motorcycle. Garrett pulled out ahead of us with a wave of acknowledgment to our existence. I knew there was no chance of him sticking around. He had said as much, but once again, how did screwing someone not entitle you to a verbal goodbye?

"What was all that about?" August asked.

My mind frantically tried to figure out what I had revealed. "Your brother is an ass."

She looked after the motorcycle, confused about what I was talking about. "Don't change the subject. Why did you not follow my lead with that guy?"

"Who, Adrian?" I grimaced. I couldn't believe she was still on about that. "Dude was hot!"

"Lenore." Oh, how I loved being scolded by my own name. "You need to stop playing the fool to all this. I didn't ask Garrett to train you so you could be emboldened by your bitterness."

I scoffed. "I'm emboldened by my new skills. The bitterness is from the scars up and down my body."

"Stop it!" August didn't yell the words so much as enunciate them in my face. I did indeed stop and looked at her. Devin and Haden divided and walked around us. They had no interest in being part of my admonishment. That was new. Usually everyone lined up to critique me.

"I know you are mad at me. That has been abundantly clear since I came back. I thought it was just because I left you behind. I get it now. I know he put you through hell. He went too far, but…" She let the word hang while she focused her thoughts without eye contact. "I know my brother." She looked at me squarely. "And I know you. If he had to go to such an extreme to get what I needed from you, then I am on his side."

"What exactly *do* you need from me? I kind of lost that somewhere in all of this."

"For one thing, I need you to grow up." I tried to formulate a response that didn't sound childish. The resulting conclusions left me silent. "I need you to start taking all of this seriously. I need you to take yourself seriously. You are important. Why do you think I keep pushing you?"

"Because you want me to be able to defend myself, so you don't always have to do it for me," I responded blandly, since I had this lecture memorized.

August shook her head. "Lenore, do you trust me with your life?"

"Of course," I stated firmly so she knew there was never any doubt of that, no matter how mad I was.

"Did it ever occur to you that I might want to trust you with mine?"

My jaw went slack and I felt the blood in my face drop to my toes. I had never once considered having to save my heroine. The thought made me as sick as giving an extemporaneous speech in my underwear.

"I don't want that responsibility, August." I shook my head vigorously. "I don't even want to be responsible for the horses." She frowned at the disjointed reference.

"Lenore, you have to stop dragging your feet. You are better than this."

"No, I'm not."

"Yes, you are!" she snapped with volume she rarely used. "Just because you don't want to be, doesn't mean you can't be! Just because you are afraid doesn't mean you get to pull the covers over your head and hide! I need you, Lenore! I need you to quit fighting me!" I searched for something on my neck to play with, but I wasn't wearing a necklace. "This evening with Adrian, you insisted on encouraging him, when you knew I disapproved of his presence."

"He was being nice. I didn't want to be a bitch."

"It doesn't matter what you want! It matters what your instincts tell you. My instincts told me he was bad news. You've always trusted my instincts before. Why did you question me tonight?"

"I got caught up in the energy. He was cute. I couldn't help myself."

"And what did you think of him after you had a chance to evaluate him for yourself? Why did you pull your hand away from him?"

I looked her over, trying to decide if she was asking to know, or asking to prove her instincts were right. "I don't know."

"Bullshit!" She was so still even though we were arguing. The storm in her voice wouldn't translate to her body. "What did you feel when you touched him?"

"I didn't like it. He seemed creepy to me." I didn't elaborate on the extent of it, but she was satisfied.

"Your instincts are strong, but they are premature. You need to start using and developing them. Garrett has only gotten you halfway to where you need to be. You need to know who to trust just by looking in their eyes. You need to be better at identifying trouble before it becomes a problem." She paused for a beat, letting the calm yogi in her return. "Perhaps you weren't attracted to Adrian Dorn like you think you were."

"What do you mean?"

"Maybe you were drawn to him for reasons other than his looks. Maybe you interpreted your attraction to him as sexual, when it was actually primal."

I shook my head and looked for Devin and Haden. They were making out by the truck. I looked back at August, trying to formulate my question. "Are you speaking metaphorically? You mean women's intuition or something, right?"

"No, Lenore, I mean you have the power to read danger like any common person might read a street sign. Stop shaking your head," she scolded even before I was aware I had been shaking it. "You are special.

I don't know how many times I have to say that to you to make you believe it, but you are."

"I thought you meant greeting card special," I mumbled.

"I need you to step up or step down. I've already spent too much time asking and begging. From here on out, you put away that chip on your shoulder and start being a first sidekick, as you put it. If you can't do that, then we're leaving you behind."

My eyes went wide and I could feel the evening's beer and hot dog start to rise. "But I need you guys."

"I know, but if you aren't going to live up to your potential, *we* won't need *you*." August walked away, knocking the last of the wind out of my sails.

Dumped

T HERE'S A SHORT LIST of reasons to stay in an abusive relationship, one of which is love. It isn't a good reason, since it means you have to love the abuser more than yourself, but for most people, love is an outwardly drawn emotion, and not an inwardly exuded one. In essence, most people are accustomed to getting their self-esteem from the people around them, rather than from themselves.

The second reason to stay in an abusive relationship is fear. Not so much the fear of the abuse, cause let's face it, at some point that becomes standard protocol, but the fear of starting a new life. No one wants to start from scratch, certainly not alone.

When August told me she would potentially leave me again, it was more than a knife in my back this time. It was a knife in my front. She was trying to be honest about what she needed from me. The problem was, she wasn't concerned with what I needed from her. Which was, simply put, to *quit leaving me*.

Despite the offer of scrunching in the warm cab, I chose to ride back in the truck bed with my coat and a blanket. It was colder than crap, but I wanted time to think. It shouldn't have even been a question. I should have been willing to be anything for August in order to stay with her, but I was starting to wonder if it was all worth it.

It was true I could defend myself now, and I could appreciate that, but apparently that wasn't good enough. Now August was asking me to do something I hadn't even imagined was possible. She wanted me to be the hero.

This wasn't the same old story about a scrawny teenager who gets superpowers and learns to be a hero. This wasn't even the story about the begrudged rich kid with enough money to exact revenge through super expensive techno gadgets. I was just me: born, bred, and fed yokel. I didn't have any ambition before the apocalypse. Why would that change after? It wasn't my self-doubt and fear that kept me from embracing this new identity. Bottom line, I didn't want to be the hero.

I was happy as a sidekick. More to the point, I was happy as the third sidekick. It was a cushy job with lots of perks. I wasn't sure I wanted things to change.

My mind was made up before we got home. I intended to move on without my friends. I could defend myself well enough not to fear the world anymore. I still had Priest as my friend, so I wouldn't be totally lonely, even if he was going to be drunk and high every time I saw him.

Without fear holding me to August, the only thing keeping me with her was love, but she had already broken my heart once. I wouldn't let her do it again. Call me crazy, but I thought leaving them would be easier than them leaving me.

With my decision in hand, the truck rolled into the driveway and stopped. I unfurled myself from my blanket as the others unloaded from the cab. Devin and August both shuffled out the driver's side. I was about to call attention to my decision when I noticed they were both looking at something in the distance. I followed their gaze and I saw it.

Fire.

Karma Smacks and Other Such Lessons from the Universe

I T WAS THE CHURCH.

I knew it even before I jumped down and climbed into the cab. Before I could start the engine, Devin pushed me aside and took over. Haden got back in the cab beside me, and I heard August land in the truck box.

Devin sped out with as much vigor as I wanted him to. He made the highway turn into a thin line with the speed he peaked at. On the last bit of gravel road he fishtailed, but was never out of control. I instinctively grabbed Haden's leg as if I could hold her down if the truck rolled. I must have been pinching her, because she pried my fingers off and held onto them until we reached the inferno.

I jumped out of the truck behind Devin, taking in the little white church engulfed in flames. The smell of gasoline was still present under the smell of burnt wood. This fire was intentional. Priest had planned to burn on Earth and in hell.

I lunged forward and Devin misinterpreted my rage as grief. Even if I was stupid enough to enter a burning building, the extreme heat of the fire would have kept me away. I strained against Devin's arms. "You can't save him! He's gone!" he yelled over the roar of the fire.

"I know!" I growled, twisting loose of his grip. I picked up some rocks from the gravel drive and threw them at the building. Most of the stained glass was already broken, but I managed to get a few clinks of breakage. "You son of a bitch!"

I yelled a long string of profanities that were in part for him and in part for me. I had trusted him to be there for me and he wasn't. I was being kicked out of my own family and I had no one to turn to.

I turned back and found the blanketed alarm on everyone's faces. They expected this would be the straw that would break me. It was, but not in the way they thought.

I laughed, trying to lighten the mood. "Boy, you just can't get a good return on the hero gig, can you? I mean really, what did I get for my time and effort, three weeks?"

I walked away to focus my mind. I was panicking and I wasn't sure how to stop it. I could take being beaten. I could take being subjected to Priest's rhetoric. What I couldn't take was being alone.

I could abide *anything*, but being alone.

I started to hyperventilate, so I sat down in the grass off the side of the drive to concentrate on breathing. August joined me. She misinterpreted my panic attack as a response to losing Priest. He might have started the spiral, but there were several more layers to my reactions.

August sat down beside me and rested her forehead on my shoulder. "I'm so sorry, Lenore. I tried to warn you. He was just so unstable."

"Please, don't leave me." My voice cracked into tears. August was surprised by my baseless presumption, but her eyes dawned with understanding. "I'll do anything you want. Just don't leave me. I don't want to be alone. I can't be alone."

August pulled my chin up and caressed my cheek. "I should have asked you what you wanted before I dragged you into all this. A reluctant hero is not much of a hero."

"I won't fight you anymore, I promise."

"It's not me you're fighting, it's yourself. You have to trust yourself. Trust your instincts. Don't be afraid to be someone important."

I wasn't sure what that meant, but as long as she wasn't kicking me out, I was content to figure it out as I went.

Angels and Demons

S EEING A GRIM SO close was beyond creepy. I couldn't bring myself to look at his eyes. The sallow glaze was the only thing that made the body look dead. The pallid flesh glittered, reflecting the moonlight, same as the snow beneath him. He roiled at the end of his leash, screaming obscenities at me. I examined the bolt that shackled him to the barn, but so far the connection was stable.

I didn't recognize him. He looked like someone I might have seen on the street once or twice. A familiar stranger, but that was all.

"Why are we doing this?" I asked, not taking my eyes off the grim.

"So you can talk to it," August answered from behind me.

"Why would I want to talk to it?" I asked.

"You need to understand what you're fighting," she said.

I turned away from the monster before me and joined her by the fire. This was day two of our enlightenment journey. We hadn't gone far—a few miles east to a different house. The residence had three grim, but two of them were babies—so to speak. We killed them and tied the third one up to monitor it.

We kept a constant vigil over him and the surrounding area. His screams tended to draw a crowd, thus the new location. In the two days we had been waiting for grim number three to start formulating intelligible sentence structures, I had killed nearly a dozen grim and August a few less—only because she was letting me work on my skills.

My training was, thus far, holding up to her expectations, as was I.

"How much longer will this take?" I asked. Our camp was starting to look like a battleground, minus the blood.

"He'll talk when he's ready." August looked over at the creature. "He's waiting to see our weaknesses. Then he'll try to trick us."

"I still don't see the point to this. Grim bad, kill grim, what else is there to know?"

"You need to know the mind of your enemy. You need to understand what their goal is."

"Their goal is to maim and kill."

"Yes, but to what end? Are they planning to kill everyone? If so, why? What happens then? Believe it or not, the grim aren't mindless zombified corpses like you think. The demons that control them have an agenda, a purpose in what they are doing. You must ask him what it is."

"Why don't you just tell me what it is?"

"Because like everything you hear second-hand, you'll take it with a grain of salt. I want you to hear this first-hand, so you can't deny it, or rationalize it away, or pretend it's an exaggeration. I want you to know the truth. Then you can understand what your job is."

"What's to understand? Fight grim, kill grim, save a few lives."

"No, that's my job. Yours is bigger than that."

"Remind me when I applied for this job again."

"The application was submitted the day you were born to this Earth. You were hired the day you were denied into heaven." She smiled, playing her statement off as clever repartee, but I got the feeling it was pretty close to the truth.

"And... don't take this the wrong way, but... why can't *you* do it?" I grimaced at how lazy that sounded.

"I'm not capable of it. Only you are."

I wanted to deny the assessment on both counts. August was capable of everything. I was still counting my lucky stars to be a pretty decent sidekick. "Wow, did you just seriously call me the chosen one?"

"Something like that." She chuckled. "You are important at the very least. My instincts told me that the minute I laid eyes on you the first time. Although, had I known you were so set in your ways, I might have settled for a different prodigy." She winked.

I smiled, thinking about the day we met. It was so special to me. That was why I loved August so much. She didn't just save me from death. She saved me from my life. There was no equating the loneliness I felt after the reckoning. When I woke and saw her face over mine, lit in a soft heavenly glow, I knew I was truly saved.

"I don't think there is a chosen *one*," August continued. "I think everyone has a purpose. Sidekicks, as you know, contribute a great deal to the hero's success. They aren't just backup. They are what drives the hero to keep going, against all odds."

"August, can I ask you something?" I asked, twiddling my thumbs.

"Of course."

"Are you...?" I couldn't believe the words I was about to speak. "Are you an angel?" It sounded preposterous, but if there were demons, why not angels? And if anyone on this earth was an angel, it was August.

I waited for her to start laughing, but she restrained herself, though the smirk on her face twisted pretty high before she could respond. "Why would you ask me that?"

"Because I feel different around you. Ever since we met, I've been drawn to you." She nodded, trying to understand. "Not in a... just like... familiar. You know?"

August looked down at her hands, remembering something. "I'm flattered." She looked back up at me in earnest. "I'm honored you could think that of me."

"Is that a no?" I asked, noting that she hadn't denied it.

Her smile grew so large that all her teeth were showing back to her molars. "I'd prefer to let you continue thinking that I am, if you don't mind. I like the way you look at me, Lenore. I like what I reflect in your eyes. You make me feel magnanimous when you look at me."

I was starting to feel a little uncomfortable by the depth of the conversation, despite the fact that I started it. "That's what a good sidekick is for, right?" I shrugged and gave her a lopsided smile.

She nodded and stared into the fire. Her lips relaxed back down to her usual warm smile. "There is something else to consider, though. Maybe I'm not projecting. Maybe you're sensing. If that's the case, then I am even more flattered."

She glanced at me, then tossed another log into the fire. A few embers jumped out of the blaze, landing in the dirt in front of me. I kicked dirt onto them, to stifle their potential.

"Would you have left me?" I asked, abruptly changing the tone of the conversation. Her brow dipped in confusion. "Before, you threatened to leave me if I didn't try harder. Would you have left me? Would you have found another prodigal sidekick?"

August frowned and tears sprang to her eyes. I had never seen her cry. To see it was like watching my own mother cry: Uncomfortable because she is supposed to always be strong, but heartbreaking because you know she can't. "There was only ever you, Lenore. Only death will take me from your side, and God willing, not even then."

I was surprised to hear her speak of God. I had never seen her pray, or use any reference to Him. In fact, she had stopped me on many occasions from clasping my hands in prayer in public. I wondered if she intended that for my protection more than any objection to it.

"God has no will here," the grim said behind us. Apparently, he wasn't a fan of the big G.

THE BIG G and the little d's

A S IF THE PUPPETEERED corpse wasn't creepy enough, the damn thing had to speak. *Chucky* dolls and rabid clowns had nothing on this demon-spawn. There wasn't even anything strange about his voice, except perhaps the clarity. The preloaded voice box had to be useless, but he managed to push his voice through from hell, along with his marionette skills.

August stilled, prepared to draw her sword at a moment's notice. I knew I should have been doing the same, but fighting still wasn't a knee-jerk reaction for me unless my life was in imminent danger.

"What the hell do you know about it?" I asked him. Snarky comments were my preferred defensive tactic.

I stood up, and August did the same. I glanced at her for some indication of what to do next, but she only nodded to me. Apparently this was my show; time to introduce myself to the players.

The grim laughed when I approached him. I checked the chain connection again. There was a slight tremor where the bolt buried into the wood siding, but it was secure. When he lunged at me, as I suspected he would, he didn't make me flinch.

Disappointed by my lack of fear, he lost his playful smile. He chanted something in Latin. He seemed wholly satisfied by his gibberish when he had finished. He panted and waited for me to do or say something. When I did nothing but stare at him, he examined me.

"Something wrong?" I perked my brow at his disenchanted inventory.

"I cursed you," he said, leaning over slightly as if he was about to puke on his loafers.

"I see." I looked back at August and gave her a confused look. She gave me the slightest head shake, indicating she had no idea about this. "Seems to have run you down," I pointed out, returning my stone stare to him.

"You are protected. Who has protected you?"

I tipped my head back with an inhalation that should have been followed by a long "*oh*." Priest had blessed me dozens of times. Perhaps he knew I might need it someday. "I suppose there are benefits to having priests for friends."

The grim glared at me through his hooded eyes. "Prayer is useless now."

"Shows what you know. I thought it was pretty useless before the apocalypse."

"He can't save you now," he declared.

"Yeah, duh, none of us are hanging around waiting for that phone call. God's number was pretty unlisted before, now it's disconnected."

"Not your god... your priest." I momentarily lost my protective sarcasm, but it was enough for him to get a bead on me. "Oh, yes, your priest has burned." I glanced back at August, but she had already settled back on her log, with her head down. Her sword was in hand, still ready at a moment's notice, but I got the impression she was trying to give me as much privacy as she could without leaving me unprotected.

"You're reading my thoughts, huh?" I asked, a little more disconcerted by that than I thought I should be.

"Did you even cry for him? Were you too busy crying for yourself?"

"Technically everyone mourns for their loved ones by mourning for themselves. It's just how it works."

"Was he... a *loved* one?" I was about to ask him if I should pull up a couch. "Did you want to fuck him?" I couldn't help but flush at that question. Before I could retaliate he went on. "Or do you prefer to stick with your sadist?" I resisted the urge to see if August caught the meaning of that.

"What the hell is your point?"

"What's the matter? Can't face your demons?"

"I'm going to let that little cliché pass for now, because you're new to the talking thing, but any more and I will have to kill you." I wiggled my finger in his face.

"Nothing you do to this body will kill me. I survive. I move on. I revive. I will eat your soul." The last statement thoroughly disturbed me, but I wasn't sure why, since it was clearly a rhetorical threat.

"So, I destroy your puppet and you move on to another crystalline dead, and then I destroy that one, and eventually you have no one left to inhabit, so you get to stay stuck in hell. Great plan, evil genius. I think if I were you, I would pack this body on a flight to the Virgin Islands where you can camouflage yourself on a beach."

The grim smirked and a guttural laugh started deep in his throat. "There are still many, many dead."

"Not for long," I said flatly.

"Not for long," he said, mirroring my lack of inflection.

"Doesn't that bother you?"

"Doesn't that bother you?" he asked overlapping my own words.

"What's—"

"—this?"

"Are we seriously playing this game?" His voice overlapped mine exactly.

"*Holy shit*," he said, speaking the words I was only thinking. "*We should sing a duet*," he suggested even as I was forming the sarcastic statement in my mind. "*Are you finished*?" I didn't bother trying to speak. I let him pluck the questions from my head. "*What the hell do you want from us, you sick spawn of hell*?" He leaned in, ready to tell me his secret. "Do you really want to know?" he asked me.

"You know I do," I answered with my own voice.

He licked his lips as seductively as he could with a dehydrated tongue. "Your souls."

"That's it?" I glanced back at August. She frowned at me, reprimanding my humor, but I couldn't resist. "I mean don't get me wrong, the whole "*brains!*" thing was way overdone, but I mean, demons wanting our souls, isn't that just... Well, it's been done—to death."

"Without your soul you will never rise."

"Yeah, I get it, we all go to hell."

"No! You go nowhere. You are oblivion. We rip away all hope, starving your soul. Your pain will sustain us until..." he pinched his fingers together, "...the light within extinguishes. Then nothing."

I stepped back from him. He took it as fear or shock and I let him. I had never thought of death in terms of heaven or hell, but I had assumed some consciousness remained. Essence, energy, or the soul, it wasn't technical; simply an understanding of physics with the weight of an entire civilization's hopes and dreams resting on it. Without the soul, death would be what everyone always feared it would be. The end.

Before I could object August decapitated the grim. I watched his head roll away with the faint disappointment of not getting to do it myself. She looked me over, saddened that I had to go through the experience. "You okay?"

"I don't know. I think I have more questions than when I started, but I guess it helps to know they aren't mindless automatons. I didn't know they could read minds."

"Human interaction feeds them. Talking to them for long periods of time is dangerous. They get in your head, as you saw. They can be difficult to resist. That's why we need to kill as many as we can. The last thing we need is them getting in so deep that they can eat our souls."

I nodded. There was nothing to disagree with. I was all for saving souls, but for some reason my instincts were flaring. August told me to trust my instincts, but she also told me to trust her. In the end, I would do as her instincts told her. After all, she was the hero.

New Roles, Same Rules

I SAT ON THE edge of the railing looking over the dirty plank floor below. A fresh layer of hay had been spread over the barn, but it still reeked from the last vestiges of bovine. There was enough room in the loft behind me to stock a winter's worth of hay, which I concluded was... a lot. I had never been in a barn this big, and frankly, I didn't think they came this big, but somebody, once upon a time, thought themselves a dairy farmer.

The dance was about as far north as I had been in years. My pre-apocalyptic travels hadn't taken me far, so I wasn't much help in finding the place. The hills in the area rolled gently, which was a nice change from the flat valley I was used to, but it did leave room for error. Danger could, literally, be hiding over the next hill.

There was a live band, which was a rare treat, even though the drummer sounded like a new recruit. There was something to be said for the bravery it took to try a new hobby during the end of days. There was also something to be said for the enduring boredom that all but forced you to open your mind to new possibilities.

Below I could see August dancing with a fine specimen of a man. She rarely let her hair down, but over the last two months she had given me more responsibility, effectively lightening her load. I thought it would be harder to deal with, but in a way I was doing the same thing I had been doing all along. I was caring for my family.

Instead of acquiring the right chips and toilet paper, I was decimating grim. Preventing intestinal distress and raw butt wasn't as glorified as killing grim, but it was still me protecting them.

I could see Devin below, dancing with a petite blonde that was playing cowgirl for the night. She even had the double-hipped pistols. He caught my eye and smiled. He mouthed, *"You okay?"*

I smiled. I knew if I walked downstairs and asked to cut in, he would have dropped his sure thing, and wrapped his arms around me to dance as long as I wanted. That was enough for me. Just knowing I could. It was more devotion than any man had ever shown me, and I wanted to keep it that way. *"I love you,"* I mouthed to him.

"I love you too," he mouthed back, drawing his cowgirl closer.

"You two make me sick," Haden snarled as she climbed up to my loft via the death trap ladder. I hadn't heard her until she spoke. That disappointed me, but given the loud music and my being distracted by my platonic lover, I didn't let it get to me.

"Why's that?" I asked when her glower didn't readily disappear.

"Why don't you just fuck each other and get it over with?" She looped her legs over the railing and pouted while she sipped her beer.

"What are you doing up here? I told you I'd watch."

"There aren't any decent men tonight. August got the last good one," she said, with sour grapes dripping into her voice.

"He is something special. I'm sure if you asked Devin, he'd forgo his evening's catch."

"No!" If she were a dog, she would have snapped at my proffered hand. "He's got someone for tonight. He can have me any night."

"Can he?" I asked cautiously. She furrowed her brow and shrugged off the foreign language I was speaking. "Maybe you should remind him of that. I mean, I understand you both enjoy the variety of a non-committed relationship, but you might find given the choice, he might still choose you."

Haden looked me over, most likely debating hitting me, laughing at me, or calling me a name. "Why haven't you slept with him? You're not still holding off because of me, are you?"

"Why are you so concerned about my sex life?"

"Other than the fact that you probably haven't gotten laid since you lost your virginity?"

I chuckled. "Almost, but not quite."

"You should get it over with, is all I'm saying. He clearly wants you." She chugged the last of her beer.

"No, not exactly—not the way he wants you, anyway."

The bottle made a kissing sound as Haden ripped it from her mouth. "What's that supposed to mean?"

"He wants to take care of me. If that means sleeping with me, then he's more than happy to do it. With you, he just can't resist. I'm telling you, if you tied your hair up, looped your shirt through your bra, and started fanning yourself like this barn was the tropics, he'd be up here in ten minutes. And the ten minutes would only be because he's a gentleman."

She eyed me again, debating those same three options. In the end, her face fell and she looked away from me. "Yeah, I guess. I do hate how lovey-dovey you two are now."

"Ahh, that's what this is about. You don't care whether I do or don't do him. You just don't like seeing him affectionate with me."

"Whatever, it's weird. You used to have a crush on him, now it's more like he has a crush on you."

"No." I tried to say it as smooth and calm as I know August would if she were there. "I'm just what he needs right now and vice versa. You're an intense woman, Haden. Any man would be happy to have a shot with you, but..." I let the word hang for a moment, drawing her eyes back to me. "Devin is a man proud of his conduct. You don't always let him... coax you out."

"Did you just call me a slut?"

I laughed, unable to contain it. When she didn't join in I held up a finger to ease her anger and cleared my throat. "No, I would never call a fellow female that. However, I did call you easy—and there is a difference." I held up both hands because it looked as though she had finally decided on hitting me. "I think what Devin enjoys about hanging out with me, is he gets to perpetually woo me. If I never give in, he gets to flirt to his heart's content, and I think we both know how much he loves to flirt."

"Who likes to flirt?" Devin asked, climbing up the ladder to join us. Haden was surprised by his entrance, but I saw the shift in the ladder this time. "What are you two discussing? Haden, you look like you're going to kill number three here."

I couldn't help but smile that he was using my euphemism about our team. He certainly never thought of me as third, and as far as he was concerned *he* was the hero, but nonetheless, he found it amusing.

"We were just discussing the number of not-so-cute men at this party," I said.

"Hey," he teased, leaning on the pole next to me. I knew Haden would bristle at his proximity to me, but from my perspective, he was leaning on the pole next to me so he could look at *her*.

"Except you, but of course that's where the debate got heated," I said. Haden continued to glare at me, but she remained silent to see where I was going with this. "With only one man for the two of us, we had to decide which one of us should get you."

"Oh, really?" he asked, his ego sitting up and begging for more. Haden rolled her eyes. She was seconds from stomping off, so I shook my head slightly to keep her oh-so-eager temper tantrum at bay. "Well, you know, you could both have me," Devin suggested. "Haden can attest to my stamina."

"Oh, she did. We were way ahead of you on that. Only one problem."

"No problem, ladies," Devin drawled, shaking his head.

"Yes, a problem. Haden doesn't share well."

"That she doesn't." Devin winked at her, and for the first time a tiny smile hit Haden's lips.

"I was concerned one of us might get left out... and Devin, I just couldn't do that to you." After a short pause, he looked down at me, confused by my conclusion. "Well, I mean, come on. You didn't think Haden would choose you over me in a threesome, did you? I mean, I'm a woman; imagine what I could do for her."

"I already am, and I know you're teasing me, but go on."

"Well, first off, I know Haden likes it rough." Haden's eyes widened; she couldn't believe how far I was taking this. "I would tie her up. Quartered and stretched, you know?" Devin added a conciliatory response to my verbal depiction, but his eyes were locked on Haden and hers on his.

I continued, knowing full well I was delving not so much into the realm of lesbianism, but perhaps one of my own late-night fantasies that was too good to actually try, in case it ruined it. "After I'd subdued her, I would slow things down. I'd kiss her everywhere but where she wanted me to. Then I'd massage her shoulders and legs. When I was sure I had her plenty warmed up, I'd…"

My pause broke the moment and they both looked at me as if I was a buffering video, and they were trying to figure out how to get me to go again. "I'll tell you the rest later. Since you guys are up here, I think I'll grab a beer. Let me know which one you choose, Haden."

I didn't bother to wait for an answer. I slipped down the ladder and waved at a few un-cuties on my way to the beer supply. I always managed to catch a few eyes at the dances, but for some reason I couldn't get the hang of sleeping with strangers. Public bathroom sex, yes; strangers, no. I had to draw the line somewhere.

I found a wall to lean against and surveyed the crowd from there. Up in the loft, Haden and Devin were already making out, and I couldn't help but be pleased with my work. I knew monogamy was a lot to ask in the new world, but I didn't think love was, and Haden and Devin loved each other, no matter what they said.

I could feel something shift inside me, and I grabbed before I fully understood what I was reaching for. On the end of my bear-trap hand I found an ugly old man trying to cop a feel. He was shocked that he hadn't managed to get a fist full of breast before I noticed him. He was even more surprised that my grip was so tight it was causing his frail skin to break.

"Do you think I should cut you some slack, pervert, because you're old?" I asked.

"Yes, ma'am." I caught the glint in his eyes, and I knew it was an act—an act of banality that had fooled more than one woman. I knew with every fiber of my being what he was.

"Did you cut those girls you raped any slack?" I didn't know how I knew, but I did. As sure as my eyes saw the blood trickling down my fingers from his wrist, I saw the damage he had done to so many happy, youthful women. His eyes were boggled at my insight and he tried to rip his hand away.

I pulled him forward, which wasn't as easy as I would have liked. Old bugger was stronger than he looked. I dropped the beer in my free hand and grabbed his chin to speak into his face. "I wouldn't want to disrupt the party by killing you, but consider yourself dead from this point on. If I see you again, I *will* kill you, no questions asked. Understand?"

He nodded as best he could and I released him. He scurried off, nearly falling before he found his balance again. August was by my side directly after. She wasn't there to defend me, but comfort me. Her new man, to his credit, came running up right after to assess my trouble and August's concern.

"What is it?" August asked in a hushed tone even though the music was enough to drown us out.

"Promise me there's a hell for assholes like that," I said.

She looked me over, baffled by the fury in my voice. "I don't know." She looked disappointed that she couldn't verify that statement for me.

"Then promise me…" My eyes were tearing up. I wasn't even sure what this emotion was. I knew it had started out as anger, but now it felt like turmoil. "Promise me that one day he will understand that he's a monster—even if he isn't punished for it, at least let him hate himself as much as they hated him."

"Honey, I don't know what you're talking about. What did he say to you?"

"Nothing. He's a worthless old man that thinks because he's old he doesn't have to take responsibility for his youth." August glanced at her new friend and he seemed to get the hint that he should leave.

"No," I grabbed his arm and instantly I felt better. I apparently just needed to feel goodness from someone to rid myself of the taste of bad. "I'm sorry. I'm being a drama queen. August, go dance with this fine man."

"Lenore, I can see you're upset. I'm not leaving you."

I shook my head. "I'm fine now. I'll be more upset if I ruin your night. Please, August, dance, have fun."

"Are you sure?"

I kissed her cheek and leaned into her ear to whisper. "He's so hot, if you don't dance with him, I'll steal him out from under you." When I leaned back she was smirking at me with narrowed eyes. I tipped my chin as if begging her to *try me*. She went back on the dance floor with her fine man and I tried not to think about whatever I had just experienced.

It was possible I had simply guessed he was a rapist based on his obvious flare for manhandling women without their consent, but that wasn't it. I knew what he had done, and for the briefest moment I could see the faces of his victims, and feel their pain.

Apparently, this was what my instincts were. I couldn't call it psychic, but only because that made it seem like a sideshow trick. It was more like a memory I already had. I only needed to retrieve it. Which brought to light a good number of other questions, but I ignored them all.

I was getting used to the responsibility of caring for my family. The last thing I wanted to add to my plate was my slow descent into madness.

The Mayor's Agenda

IT'S STRANGE; EVEN WHEN no one is technically in charge, someone always steps up to take the job. The world had essentially been cut in half. Chaos had ensued, and yet, a civility formed within it.

The *Lord of the Flies* theory presumed that without leaders and direction, we would turn into animals, worshiping false gods and taking on savagery as second nature. Golding didn't put much faith in the human species, or perhaps he just had a statement to make about parents who didn't watch over their children.

Either way, the idea that civilization would simply collapse, turn in on itself, or start resembling the golden ox scene from the bible, was preposterous. The truth was, nothing changed except our perceptions. Before the apocalypse, we all perceived the people around us as being relatively honest and good willed. Post-apocalypse no one cared what anyone thought, so they didn't disguise what they really wanted.

The only taboo left fully intact was murdering a human, and even then, if you could prove you were in the right, no one would care. We hadn't slipped back into a world where sacrifices and multiple gods were normal. We had just slipped back into the old west—when people demanded a system of law, but there weren't enough sheriffs to actually enforce it.

It was early morning by the time we got home. Haden and Devin went straight upstairs to finish what they had started at the barn dance. August was reluctantly saying goodbye to her man, but not doing a good job of it since they were both inching their way inside with each kiss.

I went into the kitchen and turned on the radio. Jimmy the Card was finishing up his late-night doting for his fans. I couldn't help but laugh at all the women out there in love with his voice. After seeing him in person, the disappointment was enough to keep me away from radio sex for life.

"Will you two just go upstairs?" I chided August.

"You know the rules, Lenore," she said with wide eyes. I did know what the rules were. They were the rules that Haden and Devin broke on a regular basis. The only reason August was quoting them now was because she was usually the one standing vigil to make sure overnight guests behaved themselves.

I moved around the island to get a better view and looked over Mr. Fine. When I touched him after my contact with the old rapist, I felt a relief there. If I was in supercharged psychic mode, I imagined I would have felt if he had dishonorable intentions.

"He's okay, August. Go have some fun. Besides, he knows he has four people to contend with if he doesn't behave himself, right?" I looked to him for an answer.

"Yes, ma'am," Mr. Fine said and went so far as to salute me, but he meant it with the greatest respect, especially since I was giving him permission to go upstairs and get laid.

August ran upstairs with Mr. Fine fast on her tail. I laughed as I went back to my radio and turned it up enough to give everyone privacy, but not so much that I wouldn't hear a scream or an impermissible struggle. I couldn't help but wonder when, over the last two months, I had turned into the one who gave the permission for guests to sleep over.

I made myself some instant coffee and sat at the table to listen to Jimmy.

"Now that my fans are settled in for the night, vacant of their raging desires, I will bring my broadcast to a close." Jimmy's voice was deep, but smooth, a hard combination to pull off. *"But before I do, it looks like we have an announcement straight down from our very own Mayor Thompson. Starting tomorrow, that's today for all you early roosters, he will be sending his military group west to collect your unwanted, inactive grim.*

"The mayor has explained in his press release that the tournaments are a resounding success and he wants to collect more grim for the upcoming events, thereby returning our state to its former glory of the good life. Wow, way to go Mayor Thompson. That man can make a dangerous, unorthodox, extermination plan, sound like a civic duty."

I nearly spat my coffee out at Jimmy's joke. He was right, of course. The mayor had a way of talking people into anything. I wasn't sure how I felt about exterminating the grim, but I did know I didn't want to have my soul sucked. With that in mind I couldn't help but agree with the plan.

And yet my instincts still flared, trying to tell me something. Until I knew for sure, though, there was nothing to do except save the world the only way I knew how: with after-sex breakfast. I pulled out the pans and got to work.

I Shaved my Legs for This

I COULDN'T HELP BUT feel giddy at going to the tournaments again. I blamed it on the excitement of August competing for her chance to win a spot in the finals with Haden and Devin, but it was clear that wasn't my only reason for enthusiasm when I arrived to the truck.

The snow had started to come down, but it wasn't nearly as cold as February usually was. However, that was still no excuse for me to be wearing a low-cut top and the tightest jeans I could find. I tried to hide it under my winter coat, but since I couldn't stand to zipper myself up in the claustrophobic straightjacket, I wasn't fooling anyone.

Even if my clothes had gone unnoticed, the makeup and carefully crafted up-do—with just enough tendrils hanging out to make it look thrown together—were a dead giveaway. I even took the trouble of donning some perfume, which in hindsight should have waited until we were at the tournament so I didn't suffocate my friends.

"Well, hello beautiful." Devin whistled from the truck cab as I came out of the house to join the others. "You're sitting next to me this trip."

Haden glared at me at first, but she seemed to lose the resolve in her anger and continued to strap down our supplies in back. August looked me over introspectively. When I reached the cab she touched my shoulder.

"Lenore..." The usual scolding question mark followed my name, but her eyes looked troubled. She must have figured out I had slept with her brother. I wasn't sure why she would disapprove, but Garrett liked his privacy, so I never discussed it with her.

I waited for the inevitable conversation where she told me her concerns about getting attached to a man I'm only going to see three or four times a year, but it didn't come. She squeezed my shoulder and ushered me in the cab without a single overly protective mom statement.

I was a little disappointed, but before I could say anything, Devin reached over and closed the passenger side door behind me. He locked the automatic lock and latched the back window. I perked an eyebrow at him, but I suspected he was only being playful.

He slid me over to him with far more ease than I would have preferred and put his arm around my neck. He rubbed his nose over my forehead as August and Haden clambered about outside trying to get in. They rebuked him and commented on the cold, but he ignored them.

"Is this for him?" he asked. I noted that he kept his lips almost motionless so Haden and August couldn't read his words.

"Maybe."

He took in a deep breath. "I don't approve," he said as if he felt begrudged to have to tell me. He must have expected me to simply give up Garrett because he said it. "He's not the man for you."

"It's not a relationship, Devin. It's just sex."

"You have me for that."

I groaned. "Devin. I don't want that for us."

"I don't want that fucker touching you. I've seen the scars. All of them," he added in case I wouldn't understand what he was saying. My eyes widened mostly out of the shock that he had been peeping at me. "I don't want him getting pleasure from you after he's caused you so much pain."

I sighed. There was no way to make him understand. "Devin, we were alone in this house for three months. He didn't beat me up the entire time. He's a slow man to get to know, but he's not nearly as cold as he seems." Haden slammed her fist against the window and swore a list of profanities at Devin. He didn't even seem to notice, or he was just immune to her insults. "You know I wouldn't be who I am now if it weren't for what he did."

"Do you... love him?" He held his breath waiting for the painful answer to follow.

"No!" I laughed at him. "Right now, I only love one man, and that's you."

His eyes danced over mine and he smiled, revealing how flattered he was. "You do, don't you?" He tipped my chin up with his finger and kissed me tenderly. "Alright, I'll back down on Garrett if you promise me you won't let him harm you anymore." I was about to offer an amused "*yes, dear,*" but he interrupted, already anticipating a sarcastic response. "I'm serious, Lenore. No more taking punches you don't have to. You're better than that now. Someone comes at you, you give them a reason to never do it again. Understand?"

I blinked away my shock at Devin being the forceful father figure to pair with August's motherly one. I nodded, unable to find a good balance between, "*okay*" and "*yes, sir.*" He kissed me again, this time less chastely. When he pulled back he winked at me and looked me over. "Well, you may not want to sleep with me, but it doesn't mean you have to start thinking of me as your brother."

"I wouldn't dream of it."

Hollywood

S INCE NONE OF US had competed in the past tournaments, we didn't know about the changes that had taken place. The glitz and glamor adorning the entrance were astonishing. The once gladiator-style event with hot dogs and beer had turned into a red-carpet movie premiere event with champagne and fancy clothes. Photographers and reporters dappled the area, clustering around familiar faces as they entered the arena.

As we approached the event center, I was starting to feel less overdressed and more underdressed. Add to that our tardiness because of the snow, and we decided to sneak in the doors with the least hullabaloo, so we didn't disrupt the festivities. Unfortunately, we didn't make it.

"Haden Summers!" a photographer yelled right before blinding us with the flash on his camera. A slew of flashes came from all around us and I was instantaneously being crushed between August and Devin.

"What the fuck is this?" I heard Haden say before the explosion of random questions left me deaf to anything but Devin's thumping heart.

As the stars in my vision faded, I could see we were surrounded by a mob of nosy reporters and paparazzi, but without such things as restraining orders and common decency to keep them at bay, we were helpless to do anything but humor them.

Haden was being smashed into Devin's chest right along with me, but I couldn't feel August anymore. I panicked, looking around for her. I tried to wrench away from Devin, but he gripped me harder and tapped my shoulder. I looked up and strained my neck to meet my ear to his mouth. "She went to register."

I nodded, feeling my panic subside, but my aversion to crowded areas was rising in its place. As if that wasn't enough, the loud gunshot not far from my head sent my heart into my throat.

The rampant attack of questions and pressing bodies stopped. The mob, now calm, took a collective step back. Haden brandished her gun high, not pointing it at anyone. Her hearty glare, however, she aimed at everyone.

"Now," she said, using her big voice, the deep throaty one that either instilled fear or arousal depending, on what words she paired it with. "Someone tell me what the fuck is going on here."

A throat cleared among the aghast reporters and Jimmy the Card stepped out. His red hair was a little chicer, and his leather jacket and jeans, though reminiscent of an 80s movie, did make him look a little less pubescent. He even donned tinted glasses, and if I wasn't mistaken, eyeliner.

"Haden," he said with a smile, showing off his broad teeth his parents had probably tried and failed to repress with braces. "This is your first debut since your spectacular win three months ago." His voice could have sold cars, won elections, and narrated movies, but for now, he was Jimmy the Card, the voice of the Metro.

"These ladies and gentlemen were sent on behalf of fans here and the surrounding states," he continued to explain. "They just want to ask a few questions and take a few pictures. No reason to offer a demonstration." He winked at her. I was pretty sure Jimmy could have talked Haden into giving him her gun if he tried hard enough.

Devin had already let go of her, and he was easing up on me. Haden looked around at everyone and slowly holstered her gun under her arm. "You mean this is all for me?"

"Well, they will report on the tournament as well, but certainly the enthusiasm is for you." Jimmy raised his hands to the reporters, single-handedly becoming the force keeping them at bay instead of the threat of Haden shooting them. "Why don't we head inside to your reserved seating, and I'm sure these fine people can ask their questions in a non-threatening way."

We exchanged looks for consensus before moving, but in the end Jimmy's forward progression was the only thing that propelled us into motion.

Walk of Fame

"**H**ADEN, HOW LONG HAVE you been shooting?" one reporter asked.

"Since I was nine," Haden responded tersely.

This was news to me. Haden never shared much of her past with me, but then again, none of us did. I had never told anyone that I had my appendix removed before kindergarten, or that I was adopted, but it had never come up. *The past is in the past* wasn't just a cliché in the new world; it was an epitaph for your memories so they didn't drive you insane.

"Will you be competing in the grand finale?" another asked.

"Of course," she snarled at the stupid question.

"Are you Devin Reed?" A reporter shoved a microphone at his mouth, nearly elbowing me in the face as he did.

"Yes," Devin said quietly with menace in his eyes. "Now get your arm out of my friend's face."

The reporter looked at me as if he hadn't seen me. I expected him to pay no heed to the request, but upon looking at me he turned sheepish and lowered his hand.

"Are you and Mr. Reed a couple?" one reporter asked, volleying his gaze between Devin and Haden, but neither answered. Haden picked up her pace and strode ahead of us, taking the bulk of the crowd with her like a mother duck.

With my view cleared I started to look around. Devin took my hand as if he was concerned I might run off. "He's probably already signed in."

"I know." I shrugged, dismissing that as the reason I was looking around. "What do you make of all this?" He gave me a noncommittal grunt. "Why would people from out of state want to know what's going on here?"

"The central states have the highest percentage of grim, but the lowest overall population. People in the populous areas are dealing with the human factor more than the grim. Most of the biggest cities are just burning to the ground, with the chaos. That's why we came here, to get away from the people."

"People are worse than grim?"

"Most days." He looked like he was going to say more, but didn't.

"And that's why you left Chicago?" I stopped walking and waited for confirmation. He stopped with me and waited for me to explain why I was giving the question so much presentation. "August made it sound like she was seeking me out. She wasn't though, right? I mean, you guys just took pity on me by taking me in."

He frowned and crossed his arms. "What exactly do you want me to reassure you of?"

"I know August wants me to be all that I can be. I get that, and I'm starting to see what exactly that means, but..." I looked at the trail of reporters that were no longer within earshot. "She keeps telling me I'm special."

"Hey." Devin brought my hand up to kiss it. I hadn't realized I was trembling until then. "Are you asking me to tell you that you aren't special?"

"Yes." I pulled my hand from him to wipe away the goosebumps I was developing on my arms. "Devin, I can't be the hero, and it scares me to death that she thinks I can. I think she's making a terrible mistake, and I don't want any of you to get hurt because of me."

"Why are you bringing this up now? Why the sudden change of heart?"

"This isn't a new emotion, Devin. I'm not a reluctant hero because I'm scared. I'm reluctant because I *know* she's wrong."

"Why are you telling me now? Why not yesterday, or a week ago?"

I furrowed my brow at the irrelevant questions. Why can't I be heard? Doesn't anyone get this? I'M NOT THE HERO YOU SEEK!

"I'm not sure what to tell you, Lenore." He shifted, drawing away from me. He was mad and not hiding it well. "We left Chicago because August said it was time to go. I never questioned it. I know you doubt her, because you doubt yourself, but August's instincts are *never* wrong."

Devin continued walking, leaving me to trail behind him. Judging by the speed of his flight, I realized I had wounded him. I wasn't sure if it was the judgment on August or myself that had bothered him so much.

Box Seats

HADEN WAS SITUATED IN her box seat with Jimmy the Card sitting right beside her. He must have been a talented man, because he was not only getting her to smile, but also to laugh. Devin was sulking behind her with his foot propped on the back of her seat.

I slipped into the walled-in box and knelt beside him. He looked down at me with a combination of anger, sadness, and disappointment. I couldn't bear it, not from him.

"I'm sorry." I hugged his stomach, and for a moment I thought he might not offer me the forgiveness I desperately wanted and needed. He sighed and stroked my hair. When I looked back up at him, the emotions were the same, but less searing. "I'm sorry," I repeated.

"You have to stop fighting this, Lenore." He caressed my cheek. "Stop thinking about yourself. It has very little to do with you. Just follow your instincts." I lowered my eyes, knowing full well my instincts weren't telling me anything different than what I had just told him.

"Whoever you were before the apocalypse," he continued, "whoever you thought you were... none of that matters anymore."

I nodded, feeling the irony of Devin using those words on me. I said those words to Priest to make him understand he was under no obligation to continue being a priest in the new world. By that rationale, even though I was a *nobody* before the apocalypse, I could still be *somebody* now.

"The person you were died that day," he whispered barely loud enough to be heard over the increasing party chatter of the event. "Let her go."

My eyes danced over his face and for the first time I understood what August wanted. I understood what they all wanted. Three months of cuts and bruises didn't enlighten me. Three more months of August's intense tutelage didn't dawn the understanding that Devin had in three words.

Let her go. Let myself go. Stop trying to hang onto a person that only exists in my memories. The world had been rebirthed in the rapture. I needed to be reborn as well.

Attempted Enlightenment and Champagne

TWO GLASSES OF CHAMPAGNE later, the sudden realization that I had been wearing the life of a dead woman the last year and a half was starting to sound less dramatic. If the champagne wasn't enough to tame my thoughts, my first glimpse of Garrett was.

He was in fine form, mock fighting his human opponents with a wooden sword. He easily bested everyone they paired him with. I couldn't help but feel pride in each of his wins. I applauded a little too loudly after each one.

He caught my eye after one win, and I smiled the smallest smile I could. I wanted to grin and wave, like an idiot, but I knew he wouldn't respond well to that. He didn't smile back, which was no surprise, but he did offer a curt nod. It was enough, enough to keep me from throwing my champagne glass at him in jilted frustration.

"So..." Jimmy's elbow slipped over the back of his chair and he looked at me. "What are you going to be competing in? Your friend is obviously going to place tonight." Jimmy nodded to August, who had also beaten her last three opponents. I felt a twinge of guilt for watching Garrett instead of her. "That will be three out of four. What about you?"

Before I could answer, Devin put his arm around me and squeezed my shoulder a little too firmly. "Lenore is going to compete in the archery tournament."

"Oh, really?" Jimmy said with genuine surprise, though I wasn't sure why. He didn't know me. Perhaps my cleavage was making me look inadequate as a contender. I smiled and nodded shyly about the admission. "I look forward to it." He smiled and glanced at my chest.

I looked away, uncomfortable with his attentions, innocent as they were. That was the problem with dressing to please your man—it also pleased other men.

I caught the eye of Adrian Dorn in the mayor's box to my left. There was an entry point to the arena between us, but no other obstructions. He nodded at me and looked me over. A small smile formed after his inspection was through. He apparently approved of my outfit as well.

He looked back at his company and nodded up the stadium. He stood wiping down his bland sweater. He wanted to meet.

I looked back at Devin. He was distracted by August and Garrett mock fighting. Neither of them appeared to be letting up, but since they knew each other so well, the fight looked like a dance more than a match.

"I have to go do something," I said before stepping past him. I thought that would be the end of it, but he pulled me back onto his lap.

"Where?" he asked, not taking his eyes off the fight.

"I'll be within eyeshot." I didn't let him continue his investigation and he seemed to know I wasn't interested in his company. He let me go and I stepped out of the box.

I met Adrian over the entryway between our two boxes. He was taller than I remembered, but I was standing on stairs the last time I met him. I did, however, remember how his touch made me feel.

This time his hands were tucked in the pockets on his pants. The only physical movement he made toward me was a slight bow. "Hello." He smiled and rocked back on his feet. He at least appeared to be nervous.

"Hi," I said, trying even now to figure out why I had come to meet him. Instincts were fine and dandy, but until I learned how to drive them, they were going to get me into some serious accidents.

"You look nice," he said, pointedly looking away after he said it. This man was not shy, but he was pretending to be.

"Thank you. I was going for sexy, but I guess nice will do." I leaned my hip against the railing in front of us and crossed my arms. I realized that it was only exaggerating my cleavage, so I put my arms down again.

"Your body is sexy," he smirked, leaning his elbows on the railing beside me so he was facing the tournament. "You've just decorated it nicely."

I couldn't muster a smile for his efforts. "I want to apologize for August's behavior last time we were here." He looked out at August. I followed his gaze and saw that she was watching us. Garrett was taking interest in our meeting as well. I didn't have much time. "She's a little overprotective," I said.

"I can see that." He sounded annoyed.

"She doesn't usually like my friends." I huffed as if I too was frustrated.

"I'm not sure we've known each other long enough to be friends, Lenore." He smirked at me again.

"What, haven't you heard of friends at first sight?" I asked, finally finding a smile for him.

"I believe the phrase is love at first sight."

"A misnomer, don't you think?" I flipped my hair back out of my face, even though it wasn't in my way. "Love at first sight. I mean, let's face it, two people drawn to each other across a room. They aren't thinking about touching each other's hearts, are they?"

His smile brightened and he stood up. I did the same, licking my lips as I did. "What do you propose then, Lenore? Should it be lust at first sight?"

"Definitely." I winked. I trailed my finger down his sleeve toward his hand. He smiled, glancing down at my innocuous flirtation. Even without contact, his proximity made me uncomfortable. I fought on and reached for his hand. It took everything I had to grip his fingers.

At first I didn't feel anything but the warmth of his hand, but then it felt wrong. So very, very wrong.

"What the hell are you doing?" Devin ripped me away from Adrian. *Shit, too soon.*

"Excuse us, Mr. Dorn," Devin fumed before he yanked me along behind him. I offered Adrian an apologetic shrug on the way. He didn't look happy about my sudden exit. Neither was I, but for completely different reasons.

Interogatous Interruptous

"**L**ET GO," I HISSED as Devin pulled me onto my seat by my lassoed wrist.

"Are you trying to get yourself hurt? August has made it perfectly clear that he is bad news. Why won't you listen to her?"

"I know and I agree with her, but I need to know more."

"What more is there to know?" He let go of my wrist.

"'Adrian is bad,' is not a complete statement for me. Why is he bad? What does he want? Is he the mayor's lackey? Or is the mayor his? I need more information, Devin."

"You're not getting it that way." He clenched his jaw tightly and narrowed his eyes, daring me to defy him. It took me a moment to realize what my flirtation must have looked like from his perspective.

I sunk back into my seat compliantly and pouted. I wanted to explain myself, but I couldn't expect him to understand what I myself didn't comprehend. I needed to touch Adrian again. I needed to read him just as I had the old murdering rapist. I needed to see how black his heart was. At the same time, I was trying to keep him on my good side in case he was as evil as I suspected. I didn't need my enemies knowing that they were my enemies.

Not yet anyway.

The Damage is Done

B Y THE SECOND ROUND, I was having trouble staying in my seat. It could have been from any number of things: The electric energy in the crowd as they cheered for their favorite competitor, the nervous prideful energy I felt watching my mentor battle grim after grim, or perhaps it was because in place of cheerleaders, the mayor had secured strippers to dance for the box seats.

Unfortunately, I knew it was none of the above. Something was wrong. The instincts everyone insisted I use were alight like a forest fire, but I couldn't translate them. It was all well and good to have a woman's intuition, but a hell of a lot of good it did with the brain of a nit-wit behind it.

I must have looked antsy, because Devin put his hand on my knee and gave me an inquiring look. I leaned over to speak over the cheering crowd. "I don't like this," I said, trying to articulate the only thing I was sure of.

"I hope not. I'm still holding out hope you'll give in someday." He winked at me and squeezed my knee before returning his attentions to his girly dancers. It took until then for me to realize he thought I was referring to them.

I looked to Haden for some counsel, but she was in the middle of an interview with two handsome male reporters.

I glanced between the dancing girls to catch a glimpse of Garrett. He was taking the brunt of eight grim at once. I wasn't entirely sure why they were bombarding him so much when there were six other competitors available. August was trying to get to him to help, but one of her three grim was too dexterous and managed to avoid all of her strikes. The other two were keeping her wary, but they weren't attacking.

I could feel myself rise as I watched the scene, but I still couldn't see the danger. August could win this tournament with one hand tied behind her back. Why did I want to run to aid her so badly? What was wrong? What was I missing?

I felt a tingle on the back of my neck, as if someone was watching me. I glanced at Adrian Dorn, but he wasn't watching me. He was watching August. He looked upward to the ceiling and nodded at someone.

I looked up and saw the gunmen prepared to save the day as the mayor had instructed them. They looked ready and willing to shoot any grim that got out of line. Aside from them, there were two new additions, but they weren't gunmen. They handled the spotlights.

My instincts, as primal as they were, were screaming at me. I stopped questioning them and let them take over even before I understood what I needed to do.

My hands gripped the railing beside me and I flipped over it. My shoes skidded down the cement wall, easing the sting on my feet when I landed on the concrete below. I could hear Devin above asking me what the hell I was doing, but I was already in motion again. Slow motion, though I knew I was pushing harder than I've ever pushed before.

Fucking legs, move! *I'm too stupid to do this damn job. Please God no! Not AGAIN!*

Despite the violation of rules, the crowd was loving my impromptu rush onto the field and they cheered all the louder. Had I had the forethought to simply warn August, she still wouldn't have heard it.

The grim spotted me right away and swarmed. I had no weapons. The first one I barreled through with the momentum of my run. The second one grabbed me and I twisted his arm, flipping him over to his back and wrenched away. The third's face shattered before me when my fist went at him full force. I didn't even feel the three fingers I broke in the process.

Garrett saw me coming through, but he couldn't get away from his grim. They were on him heavy because they knew he would help August if she got in trouble. It was all a distraction. Haden's interviews, Devin's girly dancers, it was all to keep them from noticing August was in trouble.

Adrian hadn't anticipated me. He didn't know I was still a threat to his plan. The lights above weaved in and out of the battle and settled on August. The blinding light forced her to back away from her agile opponent—back right into her lingering herders.

"No!" I screamed, coming up fast. I didn't know if I would be fast enough.

The shivs were clear glass. They were concealed so well, I don't imagine the handlers would have even suspected they were there, even if they were looking right at them. The attack would go unnoticed by the gunmen above. Two well-placed stab wounds would be enough to kill August. It would go down as a tragic accident, and the mayor would ruefully promise to do a better job to safeguard his future contestants. All the while, he would demand that we continue with the tournaments to rid our home of every last wicked grim.

I pushed as hard as I could. One infuriating step at a time.

Move legs! MOVE!

I could see it playing out yards, feet, and inches from reach. I realized that I was right all along. My greatest fear was about to come to life and there was nothing I could do to stop it. I was going to fail, just as I thought I would.

August recovered from the glaring light and sensed more than saw the danger. She spun, cutting off the hand of one of her grim attackers. The other was a hair from eviscerating her while her defenses were occupied.

He lunged. I leapt. The glass shard scraped her stomach as he tumbled over with me on top of him. We were immediately tangled in a wrestling stalemate. He wanted to gouge my eyes out, and I wanted to get off him and check on August.

I looked back. August's eyes and mouth were wide with surprise. Her weapon hung impotently at her side. The crowd almost immediately hushed in reverence of the moment. I heard the screams, but still didn't see the reason for them.

Haden and Devin were running toward us. Garrett was frantically trying to fend off his last grim.

August's third grim appeared from his ducked position behind her. He eyed me with a growl and grinned. His teeth should have been sharpened to fine points, and dripping blood, but they weren't. He was just the body of somebody I never knew.

August fell to her knees, bleeding from the cut across her belly. She keeled forward bracing herself with her hands. Blood dripped down into the sand, pouring from a different wound in her back. A nearly invisible glass shiv protruded from it.

Sixteen Seconds

A T SOME POINT, THE gunfire started and every last grim was dispatched with the precision of military discipline, including the one under me. I scrambled to August's side searching for something to do. Even as I searched, she shook her head at me.

"August..." My eyes looked onto hers, stinging with the knowledge that we didn't have much time. "I'm so sorry. I couldn't..."

She shushed me. "You have to take care of them," she whispered.

"I will. I promise."

"You have to take my place."

"I could never replace you." My eyes welled over with tears.

"You have to lead them; promise me." She looked me over insistently.

"I promise. August, please, don't leave me. I can't do this without you."

"You are so much more than you know. You have to believe that."

I didn't, but I nodded.

Haden and Devin arrived, falling next to August. They went through the same motions I had, searching for something to do, but quickly realizing there was nothing. There was only enough time for them to grip her hands and match her gaze before her eyes turned vacant and her head lolled back.

A set of stifled, whimpered and stuttered sniffles were all that we could manage to do at the moment. It was Garrett who contributed a solemn ululation of agony. I hadn't even noticed him standing behind me until then. I wanted to leap up and console him, but when his emotional roil was over, he gave me a scorching glare that broke my heart.

When I looked back at my beloved August, I noticed that Haden and Devin were giving me similarly scathing expressions. I could see the disappointment in their eyes.

This was what my training was about. I was supposed to be there to save her and I wasn't. I had failed her. I had failed my team. I had failed myself. And yet somehow through all that, I had to find a way to keep my promise to August and take her place.

Cow
Tipping
the After
Apocalypse
FELICIA JEDLICKA

Cow Tipping After the Apocalypse

Book 2 in the Nebraska Apocalypse Novels

WHILE A DARKNESS IS growing in the east, something has just awakened in the west. The Earth has been taken for granted and there is a growing list of enemies ready to take it from the depleted human population that foolishly calls it home.

With promises sure to be broken, Lenore struggles to find the strength inside of her to lead the team she formerly followed. To become the hero everyone expects her to be, she must uncover a part of herself that has long since been hidden.

Although everyone is eager to get revenge on Adrian Dorn, Lenore is certain that he is even more dangerous than he appears and she wants to learn more about him before they reveal their intentions to fight him. What she discovers, however, reveals more about her role in the apocalypse than his.

About the Author

Welcome to the mind of Felicia Jedlicka. This Nebraska native has been daydreaming plots and imagining worlds outside of this reality since her very first short story assignment in grade school. With little more than pluck and a penchant for the written word, Felicia has delved into the world of publication without a net. Follow her journey and explore the odd places and people she creates.